FALLING

NO HARM INTENDED - BOOK 1

SADRUP ROY

Made with ♥ on the Notion Press Platform
www.notionpress.com

Contents

1. 1970 Khmer Republic (cambodia) 1

2. 2016 Malaysia 27

3. 2016 Malaysia 54

4. 1970 Khmer Republic (cambodia) 79

5. 2016 Malaysia 105

6. 1970 Khmer Republic (cambodia) 133

7. 2016 Singapore 161

8. 1971 – 1976 Kampuchea (cambodia) 189

9. 2016 Singapore 212

10. 2016 Singapore 218

11. 2016 Singapore 238

CHAPTER ONE

1970 Khmer Republic (Cambodia)

Narrator: Heng Chann

I woke up at 5 AM to the sound of the rooster; there is a beautiful gleam of sunlight trying to unleash itself onto the night sky. I walk outside to fill water into my steel bucket. I wash my three oxen by splashing water over them and with branches of my coconut tree to scrub. I have done this every day since I was 5 years old. I am 27 now. I don't know how long I will be doing this. I am not married, yet maybe someday my wife will help do my chores for me. Will I get married? Does that someday exist? I do not know. I am an orphan. I still remember that day when I realized it. I woke up on that day when I was 15. I did not find my mother or my father or my baby sister in the hut, pondering for a while where they went. I cried for 2 days and walked a hundred times from my rice field to the hut, which is a mile apart, to find them on my way as foolish as I am. I never found them anywhere. One day a neighbor in my field told me that I was not the son of my mother. Those silent discussions which my mother had with my father and the hissing sound of my father when he noticed me while he was talking to my mother all seemed to make sense now. I never really felt the touch of my mother. Actually, she never looked straight into my eye.My father would sometimes try to tell something to me in the fields, and he would suddenly stop. After a few days, I began to think if he was my father, why would he leave me and go? I also learnt that we were poor, "very poor" from my mother many times. She used to give me a meal twice a day but I am always hungry, and when I drink more milk she will fight with my dad. Sometimes, I was left alone to sleep outside the house if I eat more, I liked it in a way, I can see those beautiful stars in the sky and avoid listening to my mother nudging me about my eating, until late in the night. After my parents had left, I used to continue doing my daily chores. We used to have four oxen but on the day my parents left, one of them went missing. I continued working in the field a week after my parents had left me, when I harrow the field I stand on the harrow since at my age I still do not have the power to dig into the field just by pressing with force. I stopped eating more than twice a day, sometimes when my crop fails, I eat once a day. I still have to buy milk as I don't have a cow, once I thought I could sell one ox and buy a cow, but every time I take it to sell, it cries or appears to be shedding tears from its eyes, it reminds me of my parents who made me shed tears, I go back home selling nothing and it follows me. Some people in my village say my parents left for Vietnam, while others say they left for India on a ship. Why would they go anywhere? I do not know. Some say my little sister is sick, so they took her away from the maddening sound of those American planes dropping bombs over our country every day. While others say, they are not from Kampuchea and left for Vietnam as that was their home. I listen to whatever all of them say since one of them could be the truth. I try to believe each of them on different days to console myself but one question always arrives in my mind whatever the reason could be, Why did they leave me? The oxen are now washed clear and good but not my mind, it still has all those thoughts running over again as it does every day when I wash.

I pick two oxen to take to the field every day and leave one of them at home. I may work every day, but the ox has two days to take rest in a week. I take my plough and walk towards the field.

As I walk, I see a young guy walking past me in modern clothes, his watch is gleaming with metal, his shoes were made of leather, and he is wearing a striped blue shirt which seems to be as fresh as a flower. Everything on him is years ahead of what I wear. I am wearing a straw hat, jute cloak and dirty boots. His shoes are up to his ankle and shining all black. I never went to school if I did maybe I would have also walked like him with someone staring at me.

The modern-looking guy looks back, walks towards me and asks "Hello, which way should I head over to Phnom Penh?"

"Phnom Penh?"I ask,

"Yes," He says.

I stare at him in silence as I do not know the place and I feel shy to tell no to him as he looks like an officer.

"What happened?"He asks me.

I try to say I do not know the place but am shy, words come only out of my mind and not from my mouth.

He looks at another person walking towards us and asks the

same question.

"The capital city Phnom Penh," the third person says.

"Yes," Modern man says.

"Head straight on this road, and you will come across the Mekong River where you can take a boat"

"Thank you," he says to the third person, smiles at me and swiftly walks away.

I felt elated as he smiled at me, he is an officer and many people work for him maybe. I walk silently to my field and began to plough it. The sun is very hot today and I feel exhausted already. I sit on an elevated mud boundary between my field and my neighbors. My neighbor Sorya gets water for me in his brass bottle. I thank him and drink it.

"I saw a modern man Sorya," I say.

"Modern?" Sorya says.

"Yes, he has all the things which are shining on him, he seems very rich," I say

"Are you saying you saw those white English fools?"

"No, he is one of us but very modern," I say.

"Is he Vietnamese?" Sorya asks.

"No," I say.

"Indian origin? Like me?"

"No, he is a Kampuchea born but he is very modern," I say.

"He could be from the capital city," Sorya says.

"The capital city makes everyone rich?"I ask.

"No, it gives you all the access to be rich."

"I do not understand what you are saying, anyways are you hungry?"

"Yes, let's eat."

I take some sweet potato and rice dumplings to eat. I place some of them on a leaf on the ground clear of grass as I usually do for Sorya to share from mine. He brought rice soup and noodles which he shared with me.

"What is that access?"I ask.

"Access?"

"Yes Access, you told me earlier"

"Oh, that, yes the rich people are either officer or they have access"

"If you know about the access why did you not get it and become rich Sorya?"

"Access needs training, knowledge and power, do you think I can do all that with the left side of my body going numb now and then,"Sorya says.

"Why don't you go to the hospital Sorya?"I say.

"Yeah, I heard there was a camp and they can give treatment to me for free," Sorya says.

We finish lunch and continue ploughing our fields. This is May and it is hotter than usual for us to do the work. We have less water coming to our fields from the nearby river and through rains, so our works get harder as the soil is not moist most of the time, especially now. We both struggle hard to get the work done for 2 days, we will have to plough the field again after a few weeks.

"The rich do not farm is it Sorya?"I say as we walk towards our huts in the evening after our work in the field.

"There are rich people who do farming,"Sorya says,

"They also toll-like us in the hot sun?"

"Why do they? They have big machines with huge tires to plough the fields. They also have many workers to do it for them."

"Machines? For ploughing? I never knew."

"Yes, I recollect it is a tractor. I saw it once in the capital city"

"You went to the capital?"

"Yes, I did go a couple of times in my childhood when my

father had more money, now that both my parents died I have to take care of my wife and three children I do not have the time to go."

"So you know the capital city ?"

"Not very much, I only vaguely remember."

"Come to my home once Sorya,"I say.

"But why?"

"I have to show you something," I say.

We walk towards my hut a few yards opposite the road which leads to Sorya's hut which is a mile and a half from there. We walk inside my hut, and I ask him to sit down, I fetch a pail hanging on the log which supports my hut. I place my hand into it to retrieve a bunch of notes rolled and wrapped in a piece of cloth.

"Take this Sorya,"I say.

"What is this?"Sorya says.

"Some money, my parents left it here when they left, I found it two weeks after they left and never used it, actually I never knew how or where to use it."

"Do you know how valuable this is? Maybe you must keep this for yourself it is a memory of your parents or it would help you in future to buy something or even help you for your marriage,"Sorya says,

"My parents left me with many memories, those days when I am alone crying there is no stronger memory than that. I am not sure if I can get married anytime soon with or without money, the only happiness I have is by talking to you every day, I do not see any better purpose for this money apart from using it for your health Sorya. Please take it without saying anything."I say.

Sorya takes the money and weeps, slowly he crouches both his legs and put his head in between the legs folded like a mountain and began to sob. I do not interrupt him as

I do not know what to say. After a while, I offer him some water which he drinks in a single gulp.

"I will not be able to walk and talk like how I do with you forever Chann,"Sorya says to me.

"What do you mean by that?"I say.

"Yes, on some nights the left side of my body goes numb, my wife Kala does not know this, I never told her for fear that she might dislike me or cry for me. I thought it would go away someday, and I would be normal. As days pass by those symptoms are increasing, I noticed that sometimes I am unable to speak as well when I get those symptoms," Sorya says with a faint deep voice.

"It is better we go to the camp very soon Sorya,"I say.

"I went there already,"Sorya says

"You went already? But you told me you are yet to go"

"Yes I told so, I went there for my kids and wife not to go through the pain of seeing me in this condition,"

"What did they say?I ask.

"Nothing much, I will be fine very soon is what they said"

"If they said so, why would you be so worried? I say and tend to look away from him and walk towards the entrance of my hut.

"Wait," he says.

"I do not want to hide from you, but I do not want to make you feel sad for me either,"

"Well just say it, sharing with me will only lighten your heart," I say.

"They told me I have a disease which cannot be cured in the medical camp, I have to go to the capital city," He says.

"Disease? Can it be cured,"I ask.

"They are not sure, only the doctors in the capital city can tell me,"He says.

"Let us go to the hospital in the capital city then,"He says.

"Going to the capital city is not very good unless you do not have someone who lives in the city, there are many people who rob you of your money or cheat you if they know you are not from that place."He says.

"SO there is no way out of this situation?"I ask.

"There is a way, the old lady who sells things like bangles, boots, combs and other stuff from the city in the village sends her granddaughter once in a while to the city, she knows how to read Khmer and also speak in the city dialect which raises no doubt,"He says.

"So you spoke to the old lady already?"I ask.

"Not yet, I am afraid I haven't had the needed money until now. I am worried that if my wife and kids will know that I went to the city I will have to reveal my condition which will only cause them more pain," He says.

"We will have to go to the city before your condition worsens, "I say.

"I still have six months before the condition can worsen, the doctor at the camp told me,"He says.

"Let us go as soon as possible, we will talk to the old lady get her permission and go with her granddaughter to the city,"I say.

"Okay, I am happy I told you about my condition. I can sleep peacefully now that you will know the reason I die in case it occurs, early," He says.

"You are not going to die until you grow as old as the woman who sells the stuff from the city," I say.

Sorya steps out of the hut and walks away towards his home grasping the money in his cloak with his fist. I tie the oxen to the post and put the plough in the corner of my hut. I can no longer sleep inside the hut today which only reminds me of the conversation I had with Sorya. I cook some rice for myself. I sleep outside the hut looking at the stars and imagining how far they can be, it seems like they are only a few miles toward the direction of the sky, so near. These stars would have no worry of death like me or Sorya I think so, maybe someday someone will look at the stars like I do, and that person may not know that I am also looking at the same stars which they look at since my childhood. They do not know my story, and I do not know theirs but the stars would know both of us. Maybe it is not just the two of us looking at the stars, cumulatively a million people are looking at the million stars, each having their own story of life.

The sound of a rooster crowing is sharper this time as I sleep outside, I wake up to proceed with my daily routine. I take my plough and oxen as usual but suddenly I get a thought. I put them back in place and walk towards the field empty-handed. I wait outside my hut for Sorya to cross my place. As I notice him in a distance, I wave my hand at him.

"What is it? Chann, you are not coming to the field today?"he asks approaching me.

"No, let us go to the old lady to discuss and take her granddaughter help to go to the city," I say,

"Today? No!! If we do not plough today all the effort we made yesterday would be in vain, we will have to plough the field again twice in the scorching sun."Sorya says.

"True but your condition is quite dire, we have to go"

"Let us go tomorrow Sorya," He says.

I pick up my plough and take the oxen to go along with him to the field. We slowly walk thinking about our discussion yesterday but neither of us spoke a word about it.

“Chann”

“Yes Sorya”

"Did you ever fear death?"

"I feared many other things Sorya but death never crossed my mind, had death visited early before my parents left me I would have been much happier, the feeling of betrayal is equally worse."

"Sometimes, I feel we worry so much before death and in a moment as we die all that worry is gone in an instant and any problems left unsolved would remain as is, hope God have some mercy and give time to solve the problems."

"Human problems are never-ending Sorya if God waits for people to solve their problems prior to inflicting death upon them, he has to wait forever."

We keep walking towards our fields, and just then Sorya keeps staring at a young woman who looks of Indian origin, long nose, gleaming eyes, and is tall and in splendor. She is not like anyone I have seen before in my village. She is walking across from me. I could not tolerate her absence or the thought that I may not see her any further. I was not aware of my parents leaving so there was nothing I could do about it. Now, I feel I know she is leaving, and I have to do something about it. At least I should know her name. I do not know from where I am getting the courage, probably out of desperation but I think no more, turned back and began to head straight towards her.

"Hello, Lady," I shout towards her. Her tread is quite fast so I jog slightly towards her. She hears me approaching so she tries to jog or run away from me. Seeing me going in her direction Sorya comes after me. I ignore him. I keep going ahead. She reduces her pace and places her hand in her bag to retrieve a small knife.

"Stop there," She shouts at me.

"Please do not worry, I am not going to steal anything from you or do anything to you," I say.

"Why are you after me? She says.

"I just want to know your name," I say.

"Why do you need my name?"

"I wanted to know, I thought I can never see you again," I say and before I can say any further Sorya shouts at me.

"I told you not to approach her, are you out of your mind," Sorya says.

"You told me ?"I say.

"Yes, I clearly said we should seek the permission of her grandmother first," Sorya says.

I am baffled for a moment. I could now understand that she is the lady who gets stuff from the city who Sorya and I spoke about the other day. I come out of the spell cast by the lady and wonder what a big blunder I have done by chasing her like a mad dog. Luckily, the situation was in my favor, and I was saved.

"Ya, you told me," I say.

"Both of you get away from here, or I will have to run this knife into one of your chests," She says.

"We are very sorry, I am in a critical situation and needed medical care in a hospital. I have never been to the city, and we were thinking if you could help," says Sorya

"I don't care," She says.

"Hello lady, please mind your words, talk with some respect," I say.

"Respect for you? I still do not believe you came to seek my help," She says.

I could not utter anything further. I am just afraid that this lady is capable of reading the mind.

"We are sorry to bother you, please carry on lady, our mistake," Sorya said.

I am still spellbound by her beauty and look at her eyes with full attention. I say nothing.

"Well if you are dying and need to go to the hospital, please seek the permission of my grandmother first, I will think about helping you later," She says.

"Much appreciated, you are a woman of great honor, thank you," Sorya says.

I smile at her saying nothing. Sorya pulls me in the opposite direction when I look at him and we walk ahead to where we left our oxen and plough.

"Why do you do that?"

"I did what?"I ask.

"You just tried to speak to a lady by barging into her privacy, if she informed the heads of our village we would have faced a lot of trouble."

I say nothing. We walk farther towards the field.

"When do we plan to go to the city Sorya?" I ask.

"I cannot answer that now," Sorya says.

"We will have to go early," I say.

"You liked the girl, didn't you?"Sorya says.

"Girl, who girl I am just worried about you," I say hiding my face from him.

"I know you like her. I felt you wanted to marry her the moment you saw her."

"Do Indian-origin people in our country marry native people like me, I do not think so, so why would I even think of marrying her?" I say.

"There are always exceptions," He says.

"Did you know her before?"I ask without answering his question.

"I do not know her but my wife knows her, I saw her talking to this lady sometimes at her shop while buying stuff from the city and some stuff from India," He says.

"Stuff comes from India?"I ask.

"Yes, there is a ship which comes from a place in South

India where people speak Tamil."
"Why did she frown at you if she already knew you? I ask.
"Well she seems to remember only what is needed I might be of least importance for her to take notice or as I was your friend she considered me hostile due to the way you approached her," He says.

I go to the field thinking about her every minute. She was very good-looking even when she was frowning. After a while, I think of how silly I must be to ignore the primary reason for my friend's health and walk over to propose to an unknown girl. I walk towards him to apologize for my behavior but seeing that he is busy with work I come back and again think of the girl irresistibly.

On the same day evening, we walk silently towards our huts, just as we near my hut I look towards Sorya and raise my hand indicative of a bye, he replicates the same and walks ahead. I walk inside my home only to imagine what if she lives with me inside this house, it would be a dream come true what a great relief from all the miseries of the world. I would be the happiest man ever. For a moment I believe she is with me, and I married her. I boil sweet potatoes in a bowl and feel as if she is sitting next to me and talking to her.

"Do you like sweet potàtoes?" I ask.
"Yes, I like it,"She says picking one from the bowl and peeling off the purple skin of the potato as I imagine.
"Shall we sit outside?"I ask.
"No, I am afraid of the dark," She says.
"Do not worry, there is a lot more light outside than you can imagine." I say and pour water on the twigs to put off the fire in the mud stove. I reduce the flame in the kerosene lamp by twisting the knob which moves the wick down gently. I grab a straw mat for her, and we walk outside. I

place the straw mat on the mud floor and beside it, I sleep with my hands behind my neck folded like a pillow.

"Come on, have your place," I say looking up at her. She sits on the mat with her legs crouched and her back stiff.

"Look at those stars," I say.

"There are very few stars out there," She says lacking a smile or curiosity.

Can you recline yourself on the mat? I say, a bit seriously, She hesitatingly reclines on the straw mat.

"Close your eyes and relax completely,"I say.

"Okay," She says and does the same.

"What can you see?" I ask.

"Nothing, just darkness with patches of gray light meandering in circles," She says as she keeps her eyes closed.

"Slowly open your eyes," I say.

"Two, Three no it is five, wonderful so many stars, so beautiful," She says as she begins to count and figure out the stars in the night sky.

"I smile at her gently, I told you, so how do you like it?"I say.

"I love it,"She says.

"You only love it, not me?"

"Of course, I love you, my dear husband," She says as she comes closer and tugs into my arm.

I feel overwhelmed with happiness and sleep with the utmost satisfaction I haven't experienced in a long time. I sleep through the night and wake up late at seven in the morning, ignoring the sound of the rooster. As I look at the mat, I feel foolishly stupid yet happy about the experience. I fold the mat and place it on the log inside the hut. We have nothing much to do in the field today. I take a bath, wear my cloak and walk towards the field. I do not find Sorya at the field today. I wonder why he did not come since he never missed a day coming to the field. I water both our fields sparingly. I pluck out and clear some wild plant growth nearby the fields. I walk towards my hut with nothing much to do for the day. I keep thinking of what could be the reason that Sorya did not come to the field. Is he quite sick that he stayed back at home? I try to fathom. If that is the case, he is having a hard time keeping his pain to himself and not sharing it with anyone at home. What if he is numb completely and unable to move and locked himself in his room? I keep getting all those thoughts which I pray should not happen. As I approach my hut, I re-consider and begin to walk towards the direction of Sorya's hut. It has been over a year since I went to his place. Should I talk to his family about his problem or not, what if they know the problem through Sorya and question me for not telling them? With a wavering mind, I walk steadily without any approach to handle any of those scenarios should they happen.

"How are you?"I say to Kala as she is standing outside the house as if waiting for someone.

"I am good brother. It has been a long time since you came to visit us, come inside," She says.

"You seem to be waiting for someone," I say.

"Your dear friend," She says.

"Sorry, I didn't get that," I say.

"Sorya, who else do I wait for,"She says smiling.

I control my curiosity while I began to think about where he could have been if he is not in the house.

"So you want some lemongrass tea?"Kala asks.

Before I respond with a Yes or No, she walks away past a mud wall separation and I could hear some vessel sounds from the kitchen. Unlike my hut, Sorya's is slightly big. The hall is partitioned into the kitchen and living area, and a separate partition for kids extends beyond the cover of the straw roof onto the ground outside which has sand piles scattered, which I believe Sorya has provisioned for the kids to play. In a few minutes, my drink is ready. I savour the warm lemongrass. It tastes very refreshing with a hint of ginger added to it.

"Very nice and refreshing," I say.

"What do you wish to have for lunch?"Kala asks.

"Lunch? No please, I will come another time,"I say.

"Next year? As you usually do,"

"Very sorry, I do agree I should have visited in between,"I say.

"I know brother that you do not wish to be bothered always but do remember we care for you after all even my parents passed away and I have no one here for me to talk to, I talk to strangers and people in the village to keep myself occupied from isolation, "Kala says.

"Please do not say that sister, I will visit you more often, you have three beautiful kids do not ever feel that you are isolated, Where are the kids by the way?"

"There went to the pond nearby to play, they keep asking where their father went and I do not know where he went, when I woke up he is already not in the hut. You did not see him at the field?"She asks.

"Well, I did go to the field but did not notice his presence keenly today. He may have gone for a walk nearby and I may not have noticed him I am not sure" I say

"I know where he would have gone, he is hiding something from me these days I feel so," Kala said.

In a state of shock, I am short of words on what to say next.

"I did not quite understand what you were trying to say"I say and chuckle.

"Trust me, he is hiding something,"Kala says.

"How can you say that?" I ask.

"He does not talk to me in the night after dinner, sometimes he abruptly stops playing with kids and goes out somewhere," Kala says.

"Alright," I say.

"Not just that, I know you both talk to each other daily and there is no way you would have not seen him at the field"

"Which means I am lying?"I ask.

"No, I know you are not fond of lying but to save your friend from his hideous little secret you are masking the reality."

I understand that Kala is very intelligent, and I remain silent without uttering anything further.

"Do you know what is doing in that private time of his?"She asks.

"I believe you would have probably figured it out by now, please go ahead,"I say.

She smiles at my words as admiration for her.

"He is having Tuk Tnout Choo," She says.

"Palm wine, you mean?"I ask.

"Exactly, I think, he is addicted to it these days," She says.

I feel good that I did not betray my friend by concealing his problem yet to Kala when he did not wish to, I feel better and listen further to her.

"I believe even now he would be savouring palm wine somewhere," She says.

"Did he ever go out of control, after taking the wine?"I ask.

"He did,"She says.

"Are you sure, you saw him?"I ask.

"I did not see him exactly, but I saw him walking away hastily dragging himself or limping outside the house like a fully drunk person only to return home after four or five hours. I think he does that to escape my bothering and

returns after the hangover," She says.
I do not utter a word and wait for her to finish.
"Can you do me a favor? Can you find where he is drinking?"She asks.
Again I do not utter a word until she says something.
"I have gone to the extent of asking the wives of a few men who sell palm wine if my husband is their customer, none of them said he is coming over. I do not believe them, why would they reveal it to me only to risk losing their shady business."
"I will do what I can to help your family, Kala," I say.
After a while, I feel guilty for not revealing the truth yet continuing the conversation and on top of that partially affirming a lie that Sorya is an alcohol addict.

"Convey my arrival and these for the kids," I say and give some miniature mud dolls.
"Thank you," she says as she takes them with her mind probably still holding over the conversation that just happened.
"Just a min, please take these for the boy, I know he will not be interested in the dolls," I say and handover some glass marbles.
"Thank you, you are right he is not a fan of dolls but he loves marbles, unlike his two sisters," She says with a smile glancing at the marbles.
"Time for me to leave sister, Have a Good Day," I say.
"See you brother, come over for dinner or any time of the day, I wish Sorya was also here when you came, you could have stayed for lunch today," She says.
"Sure wil return someday, I am good for today, Thank you, Bye,"I say and walk out of the hut as she accompanies me to the door.

I walk swiftly towards my hut trying to understand where would have Sorya gone. I walk over to the hut, and Sorya is nowhere. I sit inside the hut for a while and something crosses my mind. Surya's children went to a nearby pond. It has been a long time since I have gone near a pond or a lake. I recollect my childhood sometimes when I used to sleep outside and go for a swim in a nearby lake, I need no permission as no one would notice me until morning. The blue water with its glimmer in the morning shines in the night by the light of the moon. I am afraid of anyone watching me at the night and reporting to my parents, so I would avoid a dive into the lake and would do a dead drop into the lake as an arrow placed into a quiver. Prah Chan as we call the Moon and worship it in Kampuchea feels more of an ornament to me than a Lord. Prah Chan is worshipped during kadek with offerings of bananas, rice and coconut water and is highly regarded by the villagers. For me Prah Chan is not a Lord or God. It is an existence of beauty, a soulful experience. Sorya once told me an Indian legend about the moon, there is an old lady who sits within the moon. I do feel the craters on the moon as something similar to an old woman sitting crouched under a tree. The moon is astoundingly beautiful when seeing it over the river. There are some boats lined up across the shore, greenery over which the fireflies dance. The whole scene feels very harmonious and is a treat for an aching soul. I think of going to the river again and cherishing those memories again. I change my cloak for a simple shirt and walk towards the river.

"Chann, wait!!"Sorya screams from a distance on the way to the river near our fields.

"Hey, I was looking for you since morning where have you been?" I ask,

"I was at the field waiting for you, "He says.

"Really? I have been in the field a long time since you were not there I went to your house."

"Ya I came to the field a bit late, it could be that."

"Late? but why,"

"I went to see a man referred by the old lady who sells stuff from the city stating that he can provide me with traditional medicine to fix my problem,"Sorya says.

"Alright, so what did he say?"

"He is not at his house. I waited for 2 hours and came back to the field."

"Where are you heading to ?"Sorya asks.

"Nothing much, just a casual walk,"I say,

"Shall we go talk to the old lady again?"He says.

I feel very curious to see the granddaughter of the old lady again. I contain my curiosity within myself.

"Let us go," I say.

We change direction to head to the old lady's place which is 4 miles ahead of our huts.

"I went to your house Sorya,"I say.

"Ya you told me that I am sorry I would have been there to receive you if I knew earlier, "Sorya says,

"That's alright Sorya, Kala is deeply concerned about you."

"Ya she always is"

"I am serious Sorya, she is thinking you got a drinking problem."

"Well something is better than nothing, let her think about it, an empty mind is a devil's workshop at least she got something to think over."

"You do not take it seriously, do you?"

"I know Chann, she thinks I am an alcoholic probably an addict, she told me also the other day."

"And you did nothing about it?"

"I did."
"What?"
"I established the idea that I am an alcoholic"
"I do not get you"
"I made her believe that I am an alcoholic. She gave me an idea and I made her believe it as a reality."
"Okay, so you kind of used it to cover up your health condition?"
"What health condition,"
I do not say anything, and I smile at him.
"Sorry," I say.
"Come on buddy, I am joking, yes I used it as a cover-up I have walked like one and enacted as same, " Sorya says.
"She is hallucinating about your drinking problem."
"Now I can go ahead and work to fix my health if that is my destiny,"Sorya says as he smiles.
"I feel we must tell her the reality, she may feel bad but she might be stronger than we expected and help us,"I say as we are walking towards the house of the old lady.
"I am not sure about that,"Sorya says.
We walk closer to the mud house of the old lady. The house is very old, with moss growing over the tiles. There is a small square-shaped window-like opening which has a raised platform over which the lady sat. All kinds of stuff like combs, belts and bangles hanging and surrounding all around her. Vegetables are placed in from of her most of which are varieties of spinach, not very fresh, though. The lady has thick blotches of gray hair over white. She had big brown eyes and a wheatish complexion. Her face had too many wrinkles covering most of her expression.
“Choum Reap Sur,” I say,
“Choum Reap Sur"Sorya repeats, placing both hands at nose level.

"What do you want?" The old lady asks.
"Can we talk to you for a minute old lady?"I say,
"Som Peou" she replies.
"Your name?"I ask.
"Yes I am Som Peou," She says.
"So can we talk Som ?"I ask,
"Do not call me Som! " She says.
"How do I call then, "I ask.
She doesn't reply to that. An old man comes over to the front of the window facing the street beside us and begins to talk to Som.
"Keep this with you. I want results, I have gone through a lot to bring this to you, I want my children safe from the devil," He says.
"I told you not to talk to me at the shop yet you do, go away from here without turning back,"Som says giving a hard stare at the man. He walks away without uttering a word, placing the paper beside the vegetables in which he wrapped stuff.
The old lady takes the paper-wrapped content into a wooden box which I am not very sure what it is. She then burns the paper into the flame of a lamp beside her.
"Yiey, I am having a problem, the situation is quite bad can you please help,"Sorya asks in a humble tone to the old lady which he referred to as grandmother or Yiey in Khmer, I could also sense some fear in him.
"I sell vegetables. No help, go away," She says.
"We need to go to the city,"I say with a puffed-up chest.
"Need the help of your granddaughter, we do not know the city much,"Sorya continues in the same tone.
"No one is going anywhere, we all die here in dark suffering, your health is insignificant and tiny than anything you would see," she says with her eyes rolled upward and

mostly white, in a rustic tone.

"Yes we cannot make him suffer, have to take him to the city," I say.

"Go away you demon, get lost,"She shouts at me.

I look confused and stare at Sorya.

"Send him away," She shouts at me again talking to Sorya

I feel insulted, however, since we need the help of the old lady I walk away a few yards. After a while, Sorya waves his hand at me. I walk towards him. The old lady is not seen anywhere now.

"Whatsit ?"I ask Sorya.

"Hush," He says.

In a while, the lady appears again at the square platform embedded into the wall like a window. This time she feels more relaxed and calm.

"Take this young man," she says as she hands over to Sorya some leaves and something which looks like the roots of a plant.

"Choum Reap lear" thanks Sorya to Som

Sorya places his hand on my shoulder signaling us to head back home. With plausible questions still in my mind, we walk away from there.

"What is with her?"I ask Sorya as we came away a mile from the place.

"Nothing, she suggested me some herbal medicine after I told her my symptoms,"He says.

"These old women are good for nothing. They are always angry and do not seem to understand,"I say.

"I will try out today the medicine,"Sorya says.

"Are you out of your mind? You are supposed to go to the hospital, not try any random medicine," I say.

"I somehow feel she has some occult power in her,"Sorya says.

"I somehow feel you are being more naive and stupid these days,"I say.

"She had warned me not to go to the city,"Sorya says.

"It is very evident that she wanted to sell that gross medicinal stuff to you, any visit to the city would spoil her chances of you buying medicine from her, think over Sorya, "I say.

"Well I do not think she is asking me to stay back just to sell her stuff. She did not take any money or ask for anything in exchange from me"

"That is their strategy."

"You mean she is plotting a strategy for extracting money from me?"

"What else could it be ? you have a problem which she could persist for a long time with her dummy medicine and provide her money, if not today maybe tomorrow she will definitely ask."

"You imagine a lot Chann,"

"You do not think at all Sorya, maybe her Indian origin makes you trust her more,"I say with mild frustration.

"You want to hang out with that same Indian Yiey's granddaughter and are unable to control your urge to have sex with her since I stop you from hanging out with her in the city so you raise your voice at me,"Sorya says lashing his words at me like a roaring lion.

"You know what. You are possibly drunk and nothing more than a drunk idiot,"I say.

"Yes I am and you are much worse, a lone dog craving to have sex,"Sorya says.

"Yes I am alone, but I never gave up my knowledge or wisdom for some junk sold on the street,"I say.

"What wisdom do you have? Digging fields for the crop? You never raised children. You never had a family, someone

raised you and before you realize it they left you probably,"Sorya says,
"They are my parents and they did love me, what does a piece of junk like you know about my father?"I say escalating the casual conversations into hate.
"He is not your father nor they are your family you are a mongrel."Sorya says with a raised voice punching his final blow with words and left from there.
I am steadfast in the opposite direction of Sorya, my mind almost blank with his final attack. I do not know what to respond to, I do feel that Sorya is not lying to me. I slip and fall on the road as I kick my foot to the stone unnoticed. I fell down my face lying flat on the ground, the impact was quite huge as I fell flat on the ground my face hitting smaller sharp-edged gravel on the ground. I turn dizzy, I get up and now begin to run towards my home. My face is drenched with sweat and blood all over. I run faster and faster, and people walking by tend to notice me. I feel like everyone is looking at me like a mongrel as Sorya said. I do not know if Sorya is coming behind me or not, I felt so insulted to look back at him or make him know that tears are rolling down my eyes. I do not know if I am crying or dying but tears do accumulate in my eyes which do not roll onto my face. I reach the entrance of my home. The sky is very dark like a storm is going to take over anytime. I do not hear anything from the leaves or the oxen tied outside. I pick up my knife on the porch and placed it in the gap between two stone bricks of the well at the back of my hut. I kept it to protect myself from wolves or hyenas when I slept outside my hut earlier but now it has a different purpose to serve. I walk slowly towards the entrance of my hut having a hard glance at everything outside my house for one last moment. I enter my hut. Everything is still and

lifeless inside, with no movement whatsoever. All I could hear is my pounding heart.

CHAPTER TWO

2016 MALAYSIA

Narrator: Arka

If I have to say what is going on in my life, my wife is no more, or is she there? Wandering over thoughts which only add more fog to my inner vision. It would be better if I only say what is practical and happening outside me so we don't annul this journey right here. Excuse me if I breach my word and sway into emotions, it is purely unintentional.

I placed my clothes to dry outside my apartment a few minutes back. It is raining very heavily now that possibly they would have been completely wet, but I do not care about it. I like to sit and watch the rain. It started as a flower shower from heaven and ended up like arrows shooting straight to my neighbor's trousers resting on the ledge of their window. This is not the first time I abandoned my rain-soaked clothes to dry when feasible during the natural course of the weather.

I go to the coffee machine to fetch some, grab my newspaper, and stare at the rain. I get a strange thought that probably rain is always with people like a guest from heaven who meets us irrespective of whether your schedule is busy or not. You make way for it. There could have been wars on this earth when the rain just dropped onto them without having to bother about what is going on down here. When I was very young, I used to run in the rain, well if you ask me now I am not sure if I would like to do it now. I like to watch the rain play rather than play along with it. There is another player who keeps intervening in the rain quite often. He seems to be more powerful than the rain. It is the wind. When the wind arrives, the course of the rain changes and makes it quite dramatic. Rain with strong wind also instills a sense of fear especially when you hear some noises made. The howling sounds of the wind, as it passes through the grooves of my window grill, scare the cats on the street as they scream all along.

I could hear my doorbell ring, who would even want to come to my house at this time? To seek shelter from the rain, no one would come to the fourth storey of a building. Alright, let me pause my rain experience to check who rang the doorbell. As I look into the peephole of my door, I do not find anyone in sight. I go back to my chair beside the window but this time I carry my bottle of bourbon resting on the dining table made of rosewood and teak. I was born in Kurupam Village in India where rain used to be an integral part of our lives. The roof of our house was made with burnt bricks, and rainwater seeps from the gaps sometimes and drips into a small jet of water, we used to collect this water into vessels and throw it on my little brother and elder sister. After a year, my brother died of illness and my sister never smiled or played ever after his death. I mostly played with the rain alone and gradually would just watch the way it dances down to the earth. As I begin to think, without any clarity on what is the reason behind my melancholy with the rain, I take a sip from the glass with half-filled bourbon.

I recline on my chair and begin to nap when I hear another ring of the bell. Looks like today is meant to be interrupted until I part with the rain and sleep in silence with nothing to soothe my mind, bourbon or rain. I got the door a bit quicker this time not to miss the person who is as interested in meeting me as I am with him. Well, this time I do not look into the peephole to miss any opportunity caused by time delay. Well, a sip of bourbon seems to have already granted me the courage to open the door without fear or inspection. I am wrong, it is not him.

"If you don't mind, can you see if my clothes have fallen on your window sill?" she asks me. Well, why did she take so long between the first doorbell ring and the second?

"No, I am sitting by my window for an hour and did not notice any clothes as such," I replied.

She is hesitant to leave due to my expression which did not seem to give her the confidence she needed. She probably thought I may not have checked at all.

"Okay fine, Thanks." She says.

That's it, I think this is the only human interaction I had in the past twenty-four hours.

I got to my window again, this time standing behind the grill and looking at once, just to ensure that I do not feel guilty about missing something in my otherwise genuine reply to her. I lift myself on my heels to peep slightly outside the window, I could already feel the rain hitting on my head with the grudge they bear since childhood for not playing with it. I ignore the attack of rainwater jet on me only to look down and see that some dresses belonging to an age group of possibly the women at my door earlier, lying on the floor of the common area beside the play area. I quickly go down, to spot the girl on my way but of no use. I pick the clothes from the ground and go to my flat believing that either she would return to collect them or I find her some other day near my apartment, to pass on.

After a while, I hear the doorbell ring, and it is her again. I saw you picking up my clothes from my window just a while ago," she says.

"Thank you, My name is Tevy. You are?" She says as I pass on the clothes to her.

"I am Arka" she smiles at me and says "Never heard such a name."

"Do you smoke?"

"Yes, I do" in spite of saying that I hardly smoke ever.

She quickly picks a slim L&M cigarette from her pack and passes it on to me. I place it in my mouth, while she lits it with her lighter with hands cupped around to prevent the wind from putting it off. While she does that, I bend towards her with the cigarette in my mouth. Her perfume is smelling sweet, and I liked it, somehow they seem to be like the smell of little pink lilies. The smell of cigarette smoke did not seem to creep into her clothes yet today. Her wet hair reminds me of the last time I had seen my wife before the wedding. Once my cigarette is lit, she backs off to light her's which puts off my thoughts at once and I back to reality.

"Do you like this weather?" She asks,

"No" in spite that I am not sure if I dislike it, I felt insecure to reveal my real feelings to a stranger yet.

"Even I do not, I had to cancel my plans to go out today," She says.

"Why should you? You can always carry an umbrella."

"I know, I just don't like to struggle walking in the rain holding an umbrella, though I like to watch someone doing it."

I would also not like to struggle with an umbrella in the rain and only like to watch someone, but I do not say it to her yet.

"Ashtray," She asks,

"I do not have," I say.

“Fine, See you,” she says interrupting me and rubbing off the cigarette to the window frame and then taking it with her which I assume she will throw in some bin as she goes by. I go following with her to the door, closed it as she left and looked into the peephole to see her leave.

I walk to my window and with a dull thud fall back into my chair. I look out of my window moving my chair, 90 degrees towards it. I lay my head resting on my folded hands. The rain gradually fades away but the wind remains. I see a pink balloon flying and hovering over to the middle of the road. A small boy comes running after it. He takes the ball into his hands, jumps into the puddle on the sidewalk along with the ball, and randomly begins to walk back to the car beside the road. A sudden gust of wind runs through the street and the boy holds onto the thread of the balloon tied to it. The wind gets stronger, and the boy holds the balloon closer with his fingers and hand. He sees a couple of other boys with unkempt hair and dirt-painted shoes across the road staring towards him, worried that they would claim his balloon, he retrieves his pencil from his bag and begins to write his name on it. As he does that, the pointed pencil tip caused the balloon to blast. The car on the street fumbles sideways and then goes straight in a rush. The boy runs towards the sidewalk and walks away in despair staring at the sky not interested in the sight of anything else.

I watch my neighbor exactly opposite my window at the same level, who seems like an old woman in her eighties, which I could only slightly assume amidst the horizontally distorted view created by the rain tearing down the air, taking the trousers inside after all the damage rain did to it, probably they just arrived home. I could later see a young lad coming quickly towards the window and pulling the trouser from the old woman's hand and yelling something at her, which I could hardly hear. Maybe she is his grandmother scorning at him.

I go towards my refrigerator again and open the door to notice nothing to eat. I pour a glass of bourbon and sit by the window thinking of all the snacks I usually eat when having alcohol. I hear my phone vibrate to notice there are a couple of messages. I have to go to my doctor for a checkup says the message, I scheduled an appointment with them for 11 AM tomorrow. Well, I try to recollect why I did schedule a checkup in the first place, is it due to my headache? Fever? Or the loneliness which sometimes I cherish and mostly feel sad about. I need to figure out my cause before I utter something stupid to the doctor. I pick up the keys to my motorcycle, phone, and wallet. I press the button of my lift and before it arrives I rethink and go down the flight of five floors on foot. As I go towards my motorcycle, I understand that I am quite drunk already as against the law and should rather book a taxi. However, I feel like I am the soberest person right now and so I take my BMW GS motorcycle onto the highway. As I hold the clutch, I can feel my fingers sticking to the clutch and like a spark, I remove my hands from it and grab my jacket and driving gloves from the storage underneath my Suzuki Burgman 200cc maxi scooter whose keys are still at the ignition of the bike in the same parking space beside my motorcycle. I lock the scooter and start my bike's engine, rev it in neutral, and then gear towards the road at a slow speed until I exit the apartment premises. I began to cruise between 40 miles per hour and enjoy the cool wind hitting straight on my face and seeping out from the edges of my ears as I get along a stretch of road. I slowly began to accelerate to 75 miles per hour and enjoy the weather after the rain. I held onto a bridge and as I go I could see a checkpoint held by the Malaysian traffic police towards the exit of the bridge. Even in the wildest of dreams, I did not expect a check at this point in time. With no escape route, I head toward the police. However, they ask me to produce my documents, checked for validity, and then wave their hand to me indicating to go.

I was driving forth in my fifth gear and rejoicing in the cool wind, looking not once back again. I could faintly see someone raising their thumb asking for a lift. I can see a girl with blue tights and a white shirt from a distance. As I slow down to reach her, the ABS seems to have been off in my bike due to which the rear tire slid until I reached a hard stop. She asks me for a lift. I nodded in approval and looked towards the rear, directing her to get on, and as she did I started the bike and we began to move. She says, "I booked a taxi for my interview, and it had a breakdown, Lucky that I found you soon, Want to have a chocolate?".I said okay. She placed the chocolate in my left hand which I happened to lift from the handle. I placed the chocolate in my mouth with a short throw. It seems to be dark chocolate which is one of my favorite flavors. "So you have all your clothes or did you miss any?"I asked. Yes, she is the same woman I met in my apartment today."I am sorry I can't hear you due to the wind," she said. In a moment she replies back saying "Yes I did have all my clothes", she seemed to have understood the context based on the few words she grasped without loss during transmission in the wind move fast.

"Where are you heading?" I ask her.

"I have two job interviews today, and I am almost late. I am working as a freelance real-estate agent until now. I want to get into a firm," she says.

"What is the issue with freelance?"

"Well I feel insecure sometimes when I deal with clients who are much more powerful than me, they threaten me in a subtle way that I cannot deal with by myself. If I work in a firm, it will be easier and can press charges if needed and not have to pay my advocate fees. Also, the clients tend to talk carefully with respect when I am a representative of a large firm."

"So what do they ask in the interview?"

"They look into my sales stats, my communication skills, and my domain expertise and of course my licence to operate in reality."

"Are you going to put forth the reason you stated to me why you wanted to join the firm?"

"Yes I would, but I may not stress on the security part as much as I did to you. They may consider me as a liability in that case."

"So where should I head towards?"

"Jalan Imbi"

"How about the other firm?"

"Jalan Tun, around 5km from there I can walk"

"Alright"

As I was driving by it started to rain, I slowed down gradually toward the side of the road and took off my jacket, and gave it to her. She hesitated a bit but later wore it. The jacket does not have a hood to cover her head. I started accelerating my bike hard so that we can reach the destination earlier. I did feel that she was pressing on my hips tight with her thighs out of the anxiety and worry that arrived out of the speed we are traveling at. For a brief moment, I looked at her blue tight pencil-fit jeans which turned into an even darker shade of blue being wet in the rain. The rain began to pour harder when she lifted the jacket with her fingers and hovered it slightly on my head. At this point, her breasts which seemed to have floated like balloons rubbed on my back, however, they seemed to have a tipping point, unlike a real one.

In about twenty-five to thirty minutes, we reached the destination, and she got down from my bike her shoe pivoted on the footpeg.

"Thank You, I owe you a coffee," she said.

"Sure, Thankyou,"

She began to rub her hair with her hands clasping them like a sheet of paper and making gentle vertical movements making it set the way she did in the morning. With her pointed heels and blue jeans, she seemed to look very appealing for an aching heart like mine. I entered the cafe opposite her building and ordered a cappuccino since the rain had already taken out all the alcohol trance from me, the word coffee from her mouth actually made me realize I needed one in the cold weather. While they handed over the cappuccino to me, I was confused to take a call on adding sugar syrup or brown sugar or white sugar, well there is a lot of organic things going on in my life once in a while so I decided to go with the brown sugar, which states itself as organic and derived from coconuts on the sachet. I was seated on a barstool facing the huge glass enclosure of the cafe. I notice a group of people standing in the midst of the running crowd obstructing their way selectively and putting on a smile in defense explaining their latest credit card promotion. There was a short woman with stout legs and black hair. She looks well-built like a pony with brown eyes. Beside her, there was another tall woman with slender legs, a slim nose, and amber-coloured hair. I liked the short one better fit for this task to endure long hours of standing however the tall girl is able to draw the attention of people much better. There was another fair guy from their team who is chalking out something with a pencil and doing his math with a calculator he seems to be a Malaysian of Indian origin just like me. After a few unsuccessful attempts, both of them went to their kiosk and started chatting with each other. Another guy joins their team likely to be of Chinese origin and provides all of them with coffee which he brought as a takeaway. While the three are having coffee, a guy with a carton box approaches them. He cuts open the box with scissors he brought along with him and leaves the place waving bye to them after an inspection by the Malay Indian if all the things arrived as per the order. The two girls place two white cardboard packaged boxes on their desk and without moving from their place starts to wave at the people moving along their way. Initially, few of them were hesitant but shortly a woman aged in her thirties followed by an old man probably in his seventies approach them. Gradually the queue begins to increase, however, no one seems to open the box and see its contents over there. They might have been told by the staff what is contained inside the box however I seemed to be a bit curious about what was inside. I can suddenly feel someone touching my shoulder and with a slight jerk, I look back. It was her, Tevy.

"Hey, how did you find me here, what happened to your interview?I asked."Well, I am not sure about the interview, but I think it is positive."I just came by to have a coffee and noticed you sitting here."She said.

“You seem to be staring at the ladies.. ahem”

“Kind of yes and no, I am just observing their daily routine”

"So what was your observation?"

"The gift box held in their hands is attracting more customers than the entire staff over there."

"What is in the box?"

"Well I don't know I am also curious to find out, but I am not interested to talk to them now for that sake."

"Alright, see you then, enjoy your coffee."

"So what happened to your second interview?"

"Well, they said okay to hire me.."

"Great, Congrats"

"Thank You, but their pay is under my expectation so I may not join it."

"So are you heading home?"

"Yes."

"I can drop you back home if you don't mind."

"Thank You, if it does not bother you, I am fine."

"Great, let us grab a table that can cater to both of us."

We moved towards a table in a corner, and I began to take short sips and enjoy my coffee, while she is having a bubble tea. I am not sure how much she is enjoying it and I make no effort to find out.

Just in a moment, I realize that she looks a bit like Nila, my wife who passed away.

"What are your hobbies?" I ask her.

"I like music and reading, What about you?" She says to me.

"I play violin and guitar sometimes, I also play the harmonica mostly chromatic. I also love to ride my bike for no specific reason just to vent out sheer joy or mere sadness"

"That is very interesting, you seem to have strong emotions toward what you do."

"Well I never really thought about it that way, I think I am just spending time doing nothing but fulfilling my whims."

"So how do you earn? Sorry If I am going overboard about your life"
"Well I am a freelance photographer and interior designer, and I get some money from the leases of my properties back home in India. So I can manage to survive to do nothing for a few months in case of crisis."
"Well, it sounds like your work is your passion."
"Yes, and No, sometimes the more we do the same thing again and again even though it is our passion it could gradually transform itself into another stream of boredom flushing into the sea of stillness where I have spent most of the time in the past."
"I have never been to that stage yet as I mostly don't find long intervals of time to accomplish anything of other interests."
"Yeah, that is where it all begins and finally you reach a state where you end up needing more challenges to satisfy your inner self."
"Might be" She smiles at me.

We started to walk towards the parking on the way the short lady stops us, I glance at once at her stout legs which looks more muscular in close. She hands over the gift box to Tevy. Tevy giggles at me concealed from others. The stout lady introduces herself as Jenny and asks if we can provide a short survey. As she says so she also hands me a small gift box.
"Are you employed?"She asks Tevy.
"No, I am searching for Job. I have attended a few interviews today"Tevy Says.
"Are you willing to settle in Malaysia or have plans for abroad?"
"I am willing to stay in Malaysia"
"That's Great. Do you have any goals to achieve in your life,

let's say buying a car or house, studying abroad or going on a world trip?"

"Well I do not have anything planned, I just need a job for now. I do wish to buy a house and a car as well."

"That is great, so your spouse?, " She says in a softer tone however I could grasp it.

"No he is not my husband. I am yet to get married."

"Alright, we do have a couple of schemes, let me know if you are looking for a condominium or private property as your dream house ?"

"I always wanted a house on the farm, I really like that idea, however, since I stay alone I would rather plan for a condominium."

As they keep talking, I stare at the coffee on a table in the sitting area outside the coffee shop.

Three birds are watching the cup of coffee, and one of them made a gentle leap towards the cup dipping its beak into it.

A kid sips his Iced Milo alternating a nibble from his burger on the tray. In an instant moment, the myna made a quick flight and scoops a piece of hash brown beside the burger and flies securing the snatch towards the steps nearby. The remaining two birds fly towards the hashbrown and try to grab their share. The two birds get so quick that the hashbrown is done gobbling into their throats in an instant not leaving much for the bird who took the lead to get it.

"Hello, Sir?Hello"

"Hi Yes, Sorry m just thinking something, are you done with your survey with Tevy"

"Yes Sir, we are done"

"Can you let me know your details please?"

"What details?"

"Your name?"

"Arka"

"Is that your full name Sir?"
"Why do think it would not be my full name?"
"Sorry Sir.."
"Arvind Kalki"
"Excuse me?"
"Well that is my full name. Arka is a shorter form of it."
"Oh Alright"
"Are you married?
"Sorry?"
"Well, are you employed?" She changes her question sensing some discomfort in my voice.
"I am sorry, but I have something to do, Is it okay if we meet some other time?"
"Well Okay, Can you leave us your contact number?"
"I am sorry I don't remember my number and I don't carry a phone with me right now."
"Oh that's strange, good to be isolated from the hustle and bustle of daily life, maybe the lady has your number?" she looks towards Tevy.
"No I do not have his number,"Tevy says.
"Never Mind. Thank You, Sir," she says placing the gift box placed in my hand.
"Oh, by the way, I do not need this, since I could not help you much"
"Oh that's okay Sir, absolutely fine, You can meet us someday when you are free and help with the survey."
"Okay.I Will do "I say.
Tevy and I walk silently towards the parking lot.
Tevy looks at me, gives a wink and begins to open the box. Inside that there is a scratch coupon, I look into my purse and do not find a single coin.
"Your bike key?" Tevy says.
"Absolutely" I scratch the card with the key... This is a

discount voucher which can be used on any of the City Chain watch outlets in Malaysia."
"Congrats Arka, let us go shopping"
"Well, what is there in your box?"
"Well it is a water bottle.. not as lucky as you," she laughs.
"Let us go shopping tomorrow to buy a watch for you."
"Alright"
I start my bike and we head towards home. For a brief moment, I lose my mind and.

"Nila, do we have the groceries needed?" I mumble.
"What? Sorry, I couldn't hear you due to the wind " Tevy says.
"Grocer.. oh nothing, not important," I say realizing that I am not with Nila.
I come to a brief halt at the red near the signal.
"Cold Stone," She says.
"You want some ice cream?"
"Yeah, I want a sizzling brownie."
We walk inside the creamery and order the sizzling brownie. While she asks me to have some, I did.
This is the weirdest food plan I had in a day, booze followed by coffee and Ice cream.
"Arka, What time shall we go tomorrow?"
"You mean shopping?"
"Yes"
"I am free all day, but I do sleep late at night and wake up late"
"How about 5 PM?"
"Done"
We clear the bill and head home, I press four and she does on six in the elevator. We say bye to each other, and I head towards my apartment.
I open the door, take a bath and go near my bookshelf and

keep staring at the books in a row to pick the best of them. Should I re-read Papillon, 1Q84, Barkskins and or continue the war series from Alex Rutherford, I keep staring for a while and realize that I haven't fed my oscar fish pair in my 90-gallon tank yet and I walk towards it.
I notice that the filter has stopped running, so I take some water from the aquarium tank and fill it in the housing of the filter, with some noises the filter begins to work again and the surface of the water gets agitated with the incoming flow of water, everything running as expected.
I take some pellets into my hand and feed both Oscars. One is an Albino and the other is a red lutino.
I pick 1984 and continue reading where I last left it. A 900-page book, tiresome but I do not feel like quitting midway either. Sometimes the pages fly when I am curious sometimes it does not but I continue to read as we never know what is coming. I read for a while and sleep on my bed.

The next day at 11 30 AM, I hear the clattering of utensils. I walk towards the kitchen and see a woman serving something cooked for me.
She turns towards me. It is Nila.
"Come over, take your food," says Nila.
I step ahead, pick up my plate and take a bottle of water from the refrigerator and walk towards my chair.
She walks over to me smiling and curious.
"How is it?" she says.
"What?" I say.
"How are the fish head curry and rice? I learned it from my mother."
"Super delicious"
"You want some more?"
"Not yet, let me finish this."

"Alright"
"You are not talking to me much lately, am I not looking good these days?"
"You always imagine things Nila, nothing like that"
"Then why are you not taking me on your motorcycle when you go out?"
"Well you always seem to go somewhere from home when I go out, I cannot wait for you all the time, get it?"
"I do not get it. I am always with you but you do forget me and put the blame on me."
"Blah Blah Blah.. go on.. this is not new for me."
"I know you do not like me."
In a fury, she goes back to the kitchen. I try to stop her and accidentally drops the vessel with the fish head curry on the floor. She looks at the floor again and starts weeping.
"I am really sorry, it was an accident," I say.
"I know it is," Nila says.
"Then why are you crying"
"I am such a fool."
"What happened"
"Every time you talk to me. I create a mess, how would you even like my company, I also blame you for ignoring me, I don't deserve you "
"Nila, stop it don't start hallucinating now."
"You are the one always trying to control the situation, if not for you I don't know what my life would have been," she continues to sob.

I prefer not to interrupt her anymore and got the mop to clean the curry on the floor. I kneel down to wipe the floor and notice it is spot clean already. The sobbing of Nila gradually fades into thin air. I place the mop back again when a sharp headache takes over me. I got towards the fridge, emptying the left over 60ml of whiskey into a glass,

I drink it neat at once fearing that a headache can get worse at any time and I do not wish to face it now. I go towards my bed and pass out.

I stand on the edge of a cliff looking at the blue sky. Those dark clouds stare towards me ready to confront at any moment, but I do not fear them. A meandering river is flowing like silk down below. I am more fascinated by the river than the clouds which try to scare me. I am no more myself but I am the cliff standing here for a thousand years watching over the river and sky. Doing nothing, my existence is significant but not my feelings. The clouds get aggressive as I look more towards the river which defines its own course every few months crushing the new plants, only the trees survive. As I look more towards the river the clouds, get aggressive towards me. I continue to relish the river water as it hits my feet underneath, I also like the variety of fish that the river carries with itself. I can feel bricks being pounded on my head as I look down, the pain starts gradually as time goes on. I try to look above and notice that the clouds have used their last resort to gain my attention, a hail storm. The hail hits on my head hard, and the pain is heavy, I try to focus on the river and stay calm but the pain hits harder and harder every time. I have very little time but the hail keeps pounding on me. The intensity gets harder and harder. Well, I am at the last moment of my life seems to be as the pounding gets much harder, is this the end of my existence? can a hail storm demolish a cliff? Parts of me begin to give away. Each of the rocks which defines me is now shattered to tiny bits and falls straight into the river. I can feel bliss in the river as a tiny rock which fell into the river but it does not stop there yet, I look above at the cliff from the water and in a moment I also look down at the rock. The hail storm destroyed my significance but not my existence. I keep falling into the river bit by bit sinking deep into it and resting on the river bed as tiny granules of sand which once formed the great cliff. The pounding continues with great pain in my head. I walk towards my apartment door and open it.

There is a tall lad standing outside the apartment along with Tevy. I am confused, I welcome Tevy inside, and she calls him in too. I continue to think if I should ask her about the lad or let her introduce him to me. He looks quite good and well-dressed, in every possible way he looked much better than me. I did feel some insecurity as he stepped in and sat on the sofa beside Tevy while I sit opposite them.

"I don't find a single clock in your house. How do you track time?"Tevy says.

"I don't have a wristwatch either,"I say.

"You live by your own rules, don't you?" Tevy says.

"Well, I am Arka, your good name?" I say interrupting Tevy.

"I am John. I stay nearby."

"Oh is it, Glad to meet you, So you stay in this apartment?"

"No, I stay in the landed property nearby and was going for a jog I was called by Tevy upstairs to help her get your attention to open the door, we were thinking to call the police for help in another fifteen minutes, luckily you opened the door, Tevy was very worried."

I sigh with relief that he is not a threat to me.

"I am really sorry Tevy. I had some medication and lost into it," I say. Tevy looks at me with a grim face.

"Let us go out, We do have a plan, to go hang out you remember? John can also join us "I say.

"Well I do have some work at home I also need to give a bath to Ronny."

"Ronny? Your kid," I say.

"No, he is a dog, Bull Mastiff, he stinks awful if not washed in a week and it has crossed one already, so please excuse me guys, will join you again, You can find me on the Robinsons street, I am the only house with a dog signboard outside, you can come over some time."

"Thank you, John,"Tevy says.

"That's Okay, Welcome," John says as he walks towards the door and leaves the flat.

"Can I ask you something?"Tevy says.

"Sure, go ahead," I say.

"Are you smoking something?"

"No, I can understand why you ask that question but it is just some medication, that's it."

There is a sudden knock on the door interrupting us. It is John.

"Keys, I forgot them,"John says and picks them up from the table near the sofa.

We smile at him as he leaves again.

"Let us go out and do some shopping, give me fifteen minutes I will get ready," I say.

"Alright," Tevy says as she picks up some health magazines lying on the bookshelf.

There is a light breeze as we drive by the lanes at 8 PM, the roads are void of many people. The roads in Malaysia are usually clean and especially during the night, they look even better. As we approach, a signal can notice the influx of people as if they came out of nowhere. Sometimes they cross the signal like zombies in movies. There are also the rush-hour guys who seem very busy than the President they come over the last second and flash across the street with their flywheel. I drive towards Berjaya Times Square mall. In the parking lot, we smoke a cigarette and head inside the mall.

"You don't finish the cigarette, do you? I say.

"I usually when it rains or when I smoke in the open air, in enclosures I usually don't," Tevy says.

"Well, good for you," I say.

"Why do you smoke?" Tevy asks.

"I really don't enjoy smoking unless I smoke with someone else," I say.

"Which means that if I am not with you right now, you wouldn't smoke?"

"Probably, Yes"

"In that case, you should not smoke."

"Well the urge to smoke grows in me when I notice someone smoking, so In order for me to do that, you must quit first."

"Alright, I will smoke elsewhere before I come over to you."

"Well the breath of smoke also creates the urge to smoke inside me," I say.

"You are like a kid, asking too much of me" Tevy laughs.

We walk inside the mall, though I have been here earlier I am quite charmed by the grandeur of the lighting could be some promotional event as always. Tevy walks inside an essential oil store and smells some natural soap in turquoise blue colour. I wait outside since I do not like the strong smell coming from the shop. She walks back and forth examining the products and asking a few questions to the saleslady. She finally pays for something which I couldn't quite figure out from where I am standing. I begin to think about why would a woman who smokes be keen on natural and essential oil-based products, my theories of people's personalities had to be re-established. She walks out and looks at me with a smile.

"I see you have a question for me on your face," Tevy says.

"So you can face," I say.

"Not always, now maybe," Tevy says.

"Alright, I was just intrigued by your interest towards natural based soaps and oils"

"Well, it is for my friend in Singapore. She would visit me this weekend, she is a purist so this soap is for her."

"Okay," I say without asking further to keep my curiosity to myself about her friend.

Tevy walks towards the City Chain store and looks at the watches over there.

"Well you need a wall clock and a wristwatch," Tevy says.

"I used to believe the same until I met you but now that you are with me you will take care of keeping my time," I say.

"When I am with you yes, but we need for when I am not with you and when you are alone"

"You don't seem to give up on this,"I say.

She grabs my hand and places an Armani watch.

"How is it?" Tevy says.

"Well it is a quartz-based watch movement, I don't quite like the way it works, it runs on battery."

"So what is the one you prefer?"Tevy says.

"I do not prefer as such I just mentioned it is not value for money, an automatic watch self-wound or a manual which needs winding would be a better pick," I say.

"Okay, what do you think is value for money?"

"Well I think an automatic movement."

"So a watch which runs on the battery is not automatic?"

"Not really"

"What an irony, a watch which runs on the battery is supposed to be called automatic but instead a watch which

you can wind manually is called so"
"Then why are big brands selling battery-operated watches for more prices"
"Well, fashion has a price they sell it for the material used as a case and in some scenarios for the design of the watch, but there is no heart and soul for the watch though, at least for me."
"Alright I have got it since you wind the watch every day. You are bonded to it, is it so? Or is it some purist theory that you don't use electronics in your watch?"
"I think both of them, you kind of got what I am trying to say,"

Tevy asks the salesman a slim and tall man hovering above her, for an automatic watch and he walks inside without a word.

"Here it is, Ingersoll,"The salesman says.
"Well it looks quite good, but a bit heavy," Tevy says.
"So you need a watch for you, Madam."
"No, I am looking for a watch for my friend," Tevy says staring at me.
"Well, in that case, it would be fine for him Madam, however, I can show you other slimmer designs as well," he says and picks a Bering watch.
Tevy takes a closer look and says "This looks like a quartz movement if I am not wrong" and stares at me
"Yes it is," I say.
"Sorry Madam, my bad, I just took note of the slim design and forgot about the movement"
"I look at a slim Titus watch with a plain white paper dial and a genuine leather strap"
"You like it," Tevy says.
"It is elegant, like a dress watch, "I say.
"Can we try?" Tevy asks.

"Sure," the salesman says.

I try it on my hand, and Tevy liked it.

She tells the salesman to pack it however he looks a bit worried and says "Sorry Madam, this is from the couple pair and cannot be sold separately, you need to buy the female timepiece as well."

"Why did you place it separately then?" Tevy says.

"Apologies Madam, there is a new guy on boarded today, probably that is the cause, he shelved the items today, we also had a display of items of various discounts belonging to a rack misplaced wrongly."

"Is that sorted out now?" Tevy says.

"Yes Madam"

Tevy hands out the voucher I passed on to her earlier to the salesman and ask if the discount is applicable to which the salesman nods positively.

Tevy walks towards other watches inspecting them.

In a few moments, I walk towards Tevy and say to her to drop the plan of buying a watch for now and to skip over to someplace, It seems like time is not in our favour so let's buy some time elsewhere and come over some other day. Tevy reluctantly walks away looking at the Titus dress watch.

Later, we drive towards a waterfront seafood restaurant. We manage to get a table beside the artificial pond.

"What do you like to have?“ Tevy says looking at the menu

"Well, the seafood is good here," I say.

"How about oyster omelette and sea bass?"Tevy says.

"Sounds good," I say.

"How about a tower of Carlsberg?"

"Sounds great"

We get some fries along with the tower beer. We also get

two small glasses of beer into which I pour the drink.

"I really liked the watch. We should have brought it, anyways we will check out later as you wished," Tevy says.

"I do like it. It was more like the Seiko which I got from my grandfather but now it is too old, I shelved it and needs repair and servicing"

"So you have a legacy cool."

"You mean my grandfather or the watch."

"Both," Tevy says.

I smile at her. After our first round of beer, she checks her phone. Well, I keep staring at the stars in the sky to realize it had been a long time since I had seen the night sky so full of stars.

After a couple of rounds, Tevy, who was sitting opposite me, comes over and sits next to me. She is probably on a high, I could say.

"Arka I like you,"She says.

"I do like you Tevy," I say.

"Really," She says.

"Yes, I feel liberated when I spend time with you," I say.

She smiles and stares deep into my eyes. I do not utter a word. At that moment I felt she would kiss me. Just then, her phone rang, she moves her chair back to go a few feet away and attends the call.

I sat alone thinking of kissing Tevy when she returns, I keep looking at her if she is going to come over anytime soon, after a couple of minutes the sudden desire to kiss her vapours into thin air and I fill my glass with a beer sipping it, watching the stars again.

"It was my friend from Singapore, sorry I had to leave you alone and waiting," Tevy says, this time she sits opposite me.

"Oh that's alright"

"Look at those stars, every time I see them, I feel like we are living in a foolish world with our own sense of purpose which is very insignificant to the existence above, I feel exactly the same way as an ant looks at a human being. However, I also admire the beauty of the starlight and night sky which overwhelms me with tremendous joy which may not be the same as an ant looking at a human." I say
"My short break has made you a philosopher," Tevy says
"Not sure what will your complete absence make out of me" I smile
"Look over there, a shooting star," Tevy says
"GO ahead, make your wish," I say
"Well I do not have any wishes to make" She smiles
"Close your eyes," I say
"What is it ?"
"Please close "
"Alright"
I take out an automatic Titus watch box and hand it over to her.
"Titus watch? well, this looks like a lady's watch, so you brought the two of them ?"
"Yes"
"Is this for me ?"
"Yes"
"Thank you very much, I am happier you got the watch you finally liked, I liked mine as well though, looks elegant as you said"
Tevy takes my right hand and kisses it near the fingers, to express her thanks it is more of a Malaysian tradition than Indian but I did like her touch of lips on my hand.

We drive from there along the beach road, get onto the shore and sit for a while. I continue to look at the stars while she goes into the beach forging against the waves, her body is now wet slightly above the waist level. She waves her hand at me and I walk over to the same place as she is. This time I take her hand and kiss it, looking into my face she places her hands in a V shape enclosing my jawline and kisses my lips with hers. For a while, I can feel that all the stars are put to shame due to the absence of my attention towards them, I am deeply involved with the passion of her kiss. I can give away anything for these few moments with Tevy. We spend for the next few hours on the white sand beach staring at the sky and doing nothing. Maybe it was a sudden feeling of love or commitment which we have got in the spur of a few moments that our hearts have led into, each of us needs time to process this shock or joy whatever which our minds are yet to interpret.

We drive back home later, she waves me goodbye at the lift while I exit it. Tevy comes back from behind and hugs me.

"I remember something which I forgot," She says.

She takes my Titus watch from her bag and puts it on my wrist and smiles at me.

"Keep track of your time I need some of it," She says smiling at me in a soft voice.

"Will do, Thank you, Good Night," I say as I brush her cheeks with my hand.

She walks over to the elevator and it glides swiftly above me as if it was waiting for her to come back all the while.

I walk towards my apartment, opened the door and could see Nila dangling with her legs in the air and a rope pulling around her neck from the chandelier hook of my living room ceiling. The room is still and lifeless, with no movement whatsoever. All I could hear is my pounding heart.

CHAPTER THREE

2016 MALAYSIA

Narrator: Arka

I am walking in the void. I do not know my coordinates in the darkness. When was the last time I was alive? Do I have anyone for me? Am I married? Is my wife alive or dead? Where are my parents? I talk to myself as I walk into the void. A streak of gray light followed by bursts of red keeps flashing along my way. How stupid is it to live in the light, while the origin of reality is from the darkness? Light is for the lesser life, people who are masked from reality and dwelling in a world of foolishness and stupidity. Does life need to be infused into you? Is it crafting a robot who has nothing else to do but tend to his biological mess? Darkness is real, it is the origin, it is the destination, and anything in the middle is an altercation with the darkness of the void. I keep talking to myself in the void, but no one can hear it. In the void, there is no mouth. I am the only one talking, no one else talks, listens, walks or does anything here. I am new here, but I know I belong here. Bursts of white light from the outside flash inside now. The dwelling in the darkness now yells at me. I can hear them loud and clear. They do not have a mouth nor do I have an ear yet it is understood. I am one barging into the void now. The dwelling condemns me in an instant. They want me away. I feel a strong force like the way a tornado lifts an insignificant object. I am being pulled into the light. I cannot let that happen to me. I do not belong there. That is not what I am. I am not the existence of light, but I am emancipated from it. The bursts of light keep flashing repeatedly, causing the dwellers of darkness to howl at me, they try to throw me away from them but I belong to them. They channel their energy to convince my mind that light is the origin of everything and darkness is a curse, thus getting rid of me.

I can see an oval-shaped mass coming towards me at lightning speed. I try to run away from it. I run faster and faster. It comes in faster than light. This oval-shaped biological mass is cursed upon me by the dwellers. I know it. As the object approaches nearer and nearer I gradually tend to give up the truth. I start to believe the mass is my existence and the darkness is a curse. The mass now comes at blazing speeds it reaches me and keeps rotating around me. The speed of the mass is so fast that I can feel its trajectory rotating around me. I can feel that biological mass is the essence of the human spirit and is right above me, unfolding itself upon me, it pours upon me crafting my mind and the rest of my body. I can also see the trajectory which I could only feel earlier. I feel liberated, I feel joy. I feel at home. I have a path to walk to, and I control my limbs now. I feel happy as the bursts of white light agitate the darkness and variously feed upon the dark. Darkness is never meant to be. I belong to the light I no longer remember any traces of the dwellers whom I once adored. I no longer remember that I was a dweller or I adored them. The bursts of white light keep coming, and I feel a bit of inconvenience, however with my biological mass over me

I can accept it much better than the darkness of the void. The bursts of white light keep flashing. I can also hear faint sounds.

"Arka, Can you hear me, can you see me,"shouts someone from the outside of the void.

"Yes," I say as I gradually lift my chin, placing my elbow upon my eyes as the lights ahead of me are directly flashing my eyes.

"Please place your hand down, main lights off," says the man in a white cloak.

I can feel something on my wrist, so I place it down, I realize I am in a hospital and the person beside me is a doctor. A few of the lights went off, and I felt at ease looking at the man standing like a mountain beside me with silver hair on the head and a face covered with a mask. He is the doctor I suppose.

"How are you feeling now?" the doctor asks removing his mask from his face revealing a ginger beard and a pale square face.

"I do not know,"I say as I try to sense if all the parts of my body are intact.

"Okay, take some rest,"The doctor says.

"How long have I been here?"I ask.

"You have been here for 13 hours."

"What happened to me?"

"Do you have any friends or family?"

"I can tend to myself, what happened."

"Do you usually have any headaches?"

"I do get a headache sometimes."

"Did you ever get a serious headache?"

"I never got a headache so serious that I got admitted to a hospital."

"Alright"

"What happened?"I repeat.
"Well we suspect you had a brain stroke, but we cannot say that for certain as we do not have the complete details yet or your full medical history, we might need you under observation for a while."
"I am sorry doctor. I cannot stay here longer, I do have a doctor who looks after me and is aware of my medical history, I prefer there."
"Well it is up to you to get further treatment elsewhere but as you have arrived here we cannot discharge you until we ensure your current health is stable."
"Who admitted me here?"
"Someone nearby your place got you admitted here."
"May I know his name?"
"Can you check on that?"The doctor requests his assistant in a soft tone, a short blonde girl probably in her twenties, while also ensuring that I hear his request.

"When we were on the way with you in the ambulance, you were proclaimed dead by the person who made the call to our emergency department. The staff in the vehicle also confirmed the same. Miraculously you started breathing again in a few minutes. We are yet to know if the lack of oxygen led to the brain stroke or if you had such instances earlier."
"How does it matter, I am alright now?
"It does matter especially as you said that you had a history of chronic headaches."
"But it is not major as I said earlier."
"Well, we recommend that you need observation. Please try to understand that this is for your own good."
"Alright"
"Is there anything else you need to know? Though I prefer you hold your questions for later and take a rest now"

"I need to know who admitted me to the hospital."
"Can you check on that,?"The doctor asks the nurse.

I recline myself on the bed trying to reckon the day when I was last sane. I was driving along the road, stopped at the signal there was someone behind me, it was Tevy. We had an unplanned date. What happened next, I try to think but I am unable to gather all the events of the day. I badly need someone to explain, so I can sleep peacefully. I press the remote on my bed which has a call button for my nurse. After 5 minutes, no one attends to me yet. I press again and in two minutes a plumpy, chubby-faced woman, charmingly cute with pale brown eyes, comes in.

"How are you pa, odambu set ayidcha, "She says in a mixture of Tamil and English asking about the condition of my health.

"Koncham tala valikidu aana I will be fine nankren," I say that I am hoping to be fine despite some headache.

"Telugu?"She says picking hints of my accent in Tamil.

"Yes," I say and smile.

"You are informed about the medication? Are you provided with something to eat?"She asks.

"Neither, I called as I am hungry."

"Sorry Pa, Just wait,"She says as she grabs the landline near my bed and calls up the canteen to instruct them to deliver food to my room.

"Vegetarian?"She asks,

"Fine with anything apart from beef or pork"

"Chicken Sandwich and North Indian Meal," she says on the phone.

"Better you skip rice for today,"She says to me.

"That is fine for me," I say.

"You are married? Someone attending to you?"

"I am not married, no one is here as of now for me,"

"Who admitted you then?"

"That has been my question since the beginning to your staff,"I smile and ask.

"I Will check and tell you, so whom do you live with, all alone?" She says.

"I have a friend in my apartment,"I say.

"What does he do? Shall I ring him to come over?"

"No that's alright, it is her."

"Oh girlfriend," She says,

"Yes,"

"Shall I call her to come over then?"She says.

"We are not very close, it would be an inconvenience for her, anyways I am good now,"I say,

"Alright I just thought you would like to talk to someone,"She says.

"I am Good," I say.

"Alright then, press that call button when you feel alone and depressed, I usually work the morning shift and can talk to you during that time,"She says.

"Your name?"I ask.

"Shilpa," She says as she points to the name tag on her shirt.

"Thanks, Shilpa, I didn't notice,"I say,

"No worries, Ok pa,"She says and walks out of the door.

As time goes by, I begin to think if I should inform Tevy, what would be her reaction. I wonder. Being in the hospital and having no movement makes me stodgy. I tread slowly outside my room. I see the attendants talking to each other in mirth probably sharing their incidents. As I stare at them, they startle and stop their discussion right away. One of the attendants walks towards me.

"Sorry Sir," She says.

"I don't get you,"I say feeling confused.

"Well I forgot to inform you something," She says.

"Regarding"
"The person who admitted you"
"Yes, who is it?"
"Someone by the name of John,"She says.
"John? I ask confused"
"How does he look?"
"I am not sure Sir, I was only told that much from the register provided by the receptionist."
"Alright then, Thanks,"I say.
"Welcome," She says.
"By the way do you have something to read in here?"
"We have a couple of magazines at our desk Sir."
"Do you mind if I have a look?"I ask.

We take a short stride towards the desk. Almost all the magazines over there are related to health and fitness. I say nothing and grasp one of them to read when utterly bored.

"Hello, for the patient in room 108?" asks the attendant sitting next to me talking to someone over the phone
I keep looking towards anything else I can read as I surf through the pile of magazines which lay over there. I see a nat geo magazine and pick it up.
"Hi Sir, there is a visitor for you by the name of John can we ask him to come over now," the attendant now asks me placing a hand over the phone.
"Should be fine, who is it by the way?"I ask.
"John," she says.
"I feel sick staying in the room all day is it possible I can meet him outside instead,"I ask.
"I am afraid we cannot allow you for that Sir," She says.
"Okay let him come over," I say.
"I heard you, went for a while,"Shilpa says walking gradually from behind into my sight
"Thank you, Shilpa, Good to see you,"I say.

"Patient is coming towards reception please inform the visitor to stay there for a few minutes," she says over the phone.

I walk towards my room, combed my hair, and changed into shorts and a Polo T-shirt. I go outside my room.

"Hello smart one," says Shilpa and laughs at me

I smile at her, there is some natural vibe about her, makes me feel at ease in spite that it is just the third time I am looking at her.

I walk towards the lift and press 1, led turns blue from amber. As I walk towards the reception, I recollect that I met this man before, he is the same tall guy who came to my apartment with Tevy when I am locked inside sleeping.

"Hello Sir,"I say as I walk towards him offering a handshake. He is well dressed in a white formal shirt and in black thin stripe trousers, possibly he kept his suit in his car.

"Hello, how are you?" He says with a handshake.

"You gave me relief, I could bargain some air that you are here,"I say.

"I am sorry I could not meet you earlier, strangely you do not carry a phone and I could not catch up with you,"He says smiling.

"I am sorry for that. I need to get one. I did not have many friends nor did I have a job so I never felt the need for it,"I say.

"Cool, I doubt if there is anyone else having this luxury like you, we are slaves to our devices," He says and smiles,

"I came straight from the office, so," He says as he shrugs.

"That's alright much better than the hospital apron I was in a few moments until you came here,"I say.

We walk towards the hospital entrance as everyone is busy with their work and does not bother to notice us.

"So where do you work, I ask him?"
"I work for JK construction as an architect."
"Nice"
"How about you"
"I am a photographer, also did some interior designs in the past and I do get some money from property rental for now."
"You have earned a lot then."
"Not really, I inherited some land in India which by luck turned into a hot cake in ten years, I gave it for construction from my savings and was able to survive from the rentals."
"Great you should get into some business."
"Well, no offense but am not particularly interested in hoarding money," I say.
"Alright," He says looking at his watch probably not quite amused with the statement I made about money.
"I have one thing to ask, how did I end up here."
"Well that is a long story, and I feel a small shiver to rethink it, you have slept in the garden in the common area of your apartment."
"And then?"I ask as I try to recollect.
"There was a heavy downpour of rain on you, and you did not move even the slightest bit, the strange part was there was a hail storm pulling over and since it was late in the night nobody has noticed you probably everyone is locked inside. I brought you under shelter only to notice that you were completely unconscious, you did not even shiver. I tried to wake you up, but you gave no response. I called the ambulance and sat beside you at the vehicle's rear. At one point, I thought you were dead, so I checked your breath, and it stopped. Even when we arrived at the hospital your breath stopped, and the staff considered you dead. Only after a couple of minutes, you did move your fingers which

were noticed by some visitor in the hospital looking at you and then they used a defibrillator to spring you back to life."John says,

"I just cannot say how much I owe you, John,"I say.

"That is alright John."

"This is probably the second time you have come to my rescue."

"No, the first time you just took medication and we barged in, nothing I have done, by the way, how is Tevy? She was worried for you on the day you were locked in, did you call her after you got admitted here?"

"I do not have a mobile with me nor do I have her number to call, we were just being close friends very recently and this happened. I doubt if I should tell this now to her, in any case, I will be discharged soon."

"You seriously need to reconsider your decision to keep a phone. Tevy would probably be worried that you are not in your apartment. I know that woman and the look in her eyes the day you were stuck in your flat, trust me she has very strong feelings for you, I would rather not say but she probably likes you more than you know."

"Thank you, John, I will get a phone. I will inform Tevy"I say.

"Though I could stay for some more time, I do not wish to disturb you as you should take some rest now, Good-bye."

"Bye John, I am grateful for all the help once again," I say.

John salutes and leaves. I begin to think of Tevy now. Should I tell her or let these days pass by and explain later? I reckon.

I walk back to the hospital to resume my sedentary life. As I approach the floor, I could see everyone near my room. Feels like something has escalated. They are probably expecting me. Shilpa is looking at me with a deliberate smile on her face.

"Where have you been so long?" She asks in a subdued voice.

"I just went for a walk outside the hospital, I thought we were cool about it,"I say.

"Well the CEO, senior doctors and surgeons came for an auditory visit to the ward and you were the only patient missing, they ran through all names in the register. I am still not sure if I would be suspended or not,"Shilpa says softly to me.

All the attendees are near Shilpa concerned. I say sorry to Shilpa and walk towards my room. I quickly change into my apron and stay on the bed doing nothing. I hear some commotion outside my room, so I open the door and check, it is the senior staff who was doing the audit. One of them, a tall caucasian woman in a black suit whose dress code seems odd to the hospital atmosphere walks across the balcony towards the staff. The attendant makes a moustache sign at me with their hands indicating some importance to her as their boss.

I call out Shilpa which also catches the attention of the lady in a suit to look at me.

"Where did you go young man?" asks the boss

"Well I was feeling claustrophobic couldn't take it at all and had a splitting headache on top of it. I have asked the staff, and they have denied my request."

"You denied that request?" she asks Shilpa with a quick glance towards the other attendants as well.

"We did Mam," they say.

"Why? Did you manage to talk to the patient Mr?"she tells them and asks me.

"Arka," I say.

"Did you check on Arka's concern?" she asks the staff.

"Yes they did, Shilpa did, I am very grateful for that, I feel much better now after a short stride away from the reception," I say without raising an alarm though I am a bit skeptical of her response.

"Good work Shilpa," she says to her.

"Shilpa keeps it up. We should hear the patients as you did, it is a thin line and you understood well," says another senior doctor to her, standing between the lady in the suit and the staff.

Shortly all of them leave and I feel good that at least now I know she is saved for the day. However, Shilpa is not all smiles again, she does hold some frustration towards me not very evident but exists.

After a while, in my room, I am reading the nat geo magazine on rescuing sea life, especially sharks. The article details shark finning how it is executed and its impact on sharks. Some humans tend to slice off shark fins for soup and traditional medicine. Sharks after their fins are cut off cannot propel forth and usually sink to the rump of the ocean and die gradually. I close my eyes looking at the bottom of the sea where a lone shark who scared the shit out of smaller fish and fed on them is now rocking back and forth helplessly. Those small fish, lured by blood oozing from the injury of the shark, feeds on her when she is still alive. There exists in a state between death and the acceptance of death to dawn upon oneself, if it ever occurs, I would say that is the strongest emotion of life and the bravest moment an individual endures.

Nila was stuck in that state, she never accepted death despite losing her body like the lost fins. She is fighting like a shark. I am on the ocean floor looking at her. I cannot grow her fins nor can I kill her. I have to move on, but that would be the most gruesome act ever done. I never loved her to the extent that she did to me. I always acknowledged her love, never reciprocating it much. Her love is beyond death. I know she can never succumb to the mediocrity of death. If it does ever happen, she will still reign over it. Her emotions were much strong. I still do not know how Nila could exist past death. Right now she is inside my mind. My thoughts are the reflections of her desire. I know I cannot analyze this state of mind with clarity when she is dwelling in my mind, as then she takes hold of my thoughts in a fist, not one to seep out without her mindfulness. The palpitations of my heart are an indication of her exertion over my mind. I wish I could take over my mind. I can wish to do so, but it is seemingly impossible with Nila swaying like the shark in my head. She is fending off those independent thoughts of mine to get away from her and live a life of my own.

Someone knocks on my door,

"Hello, please come inside,"I say.

"How are you Pa?"Shilpa asks.

"I am good just reading some magazine,"I say.

"Okay great, so what is it you are reading?"She asks.

"Nat Geo magazine, that is the only one I found interesting among all the health stuffs," I say.

"Okay, finally, you are interested to do something here," She says.

"Yeah but it is still not a book, I would be bored again by tomorrow,"I say.

"Not to worry, I will check for previous publications of the same magazine to our hospital and pass it on, anyways that stuff does not get outdated like news"

"Alright thank you very much. You are very accommodative to my requests,"I say.

"Good half of the patients here are not required to be

treated like the way we do, when it comes to mind I believe that some dosage of freedom is the best thing a doctor can give,"She says.

"I second that,"I say.

"There are few exceptions though. We cannot grant freedom to people who are completely insane like a wiring problem in their mind," She says.

"So what do you do about them?"I ask.

"Earn as much as you can and wait till they die,"She says.

"That is a very bold and careless answer from medical staff,"I say.

"Truth is always like that, there is nothing you can do to an insane mind apart from latching it to slow down or ultimately shutting down,"She says.

"What about people stuck between sanity and insanity," I ask.

"Well if I knew that I would have been a doctor,"She says and smiles witty handing over my daily dose of pills.

I cease to remember what I was doing a few moments earlier. I feel some nausea within me. I rest along the bed reclining it horizontally. Tevy her perfect body a very hot woman, she asked me for a ride in the rain and I could not resist. At that moment there was freedom in my mind. It could do whatever it wanted to. I continue to think of her with an erection. I walk towards the bathroom in my white apron and place my plastic flip-flops outside the door. I walk inside still thinking of her wet body in the rain. I open the shower with lukewarm water hitting my penis imagining her holding it. I unleash my erotic imagination. In a few minutes, my craving has suspended with my job done. I clean all the mess with a hand flush and re-open the shower again for its real purpose, to take a bath. I lay down on the bed sleeping for the next five hours with my mind like a black hole absorbing every possible thought that comes over, thoughts innovated and recreated into another parallel world or simply put together, a dream.

On the following day morning, I am having some breakfast provided to me probably placed on the table while I am asleep. I am not sure if I locked or unlocked it and left the door open for them to come over. I have my croissant and scrambled egg. I place the leftovers and plastic wrap in the trash bin outside my room. I walk towards the reception.

"Is Shilpa in today?"I ask.

"No, she is working the afternoon shift today."

The attendant a short Chinese woman with a pale, wrinkled face probably in her thirties says to me.

"Alright," I say.

As I walk away from the woman, I can hear the attendants giggling. Probably they are amused by the thought that I am asking for Shilpa itself. Young ladies find amusement in every single view they derive from conversations I suppose. If not for such entertainment they cannot fight boredom when idle.

I change myself into shorts determined to leave the hospital. I can no longer take the boredom and sit over here. I am not sure if I have a medical condition but I am sure I will go insane sitting in that room all day long. I take the lift sneaking into the right moment when there is fewer staff. I walk towards the reception tucking myself in the crowd and proceed towards the road. After half a mile of walking, I wave my hand to a taxi and proceed home. I feel a great sense of freedom finally.

"Can I smoke?"I ask the driver.

"I usually do not allow, but that's okay Sir please do," He says.

"Thank you, do you mind a lighter and a cigarette? You can include it in my bill?I say.
"No worries Sir, please take it," he says as he points at the dashboard smiling at my strange request.
I pick one from his almost full pack and light it with his zippo.
"Where are you coming from?"He asks me.
"Just from the point where you picked me up,"I say.
"You are a very funny and strange person," He laughs at me.
"So, you drive all day?"I ask.
"No Sir, I drive only at the night, today is special it is my 20th wedding anniversary so we planned for dinner," He says.
"Congrats, have a great time,"I say staring at the person more closely now than before, he is a typical Malaysian man probably a Muslim as I see a white self-design headwrap in the glovebox of his car.
"Are you married, Sir?" He asks.
"Yes and No,"I say.
"You haven't given me a simple answer till now Sir,"He says as he bursts into laughter.
"Nothing like that, that is the answer to your question, I was married but"
"But you got divorced?"He says interrupting my question.
"Yes, you are correct," I say feeling more comfortable putting it that way rather than detailing the death of my wife to some stranger.
"Right"
"Sorry Sir"
"Right, you need to take the next right into the fifth avenue."
"Oh okay"
The Yellow Toyota veers into the street on the right and then moves swiftly.

"Right there into that parking lot,"I say.

"How much"

"120 ringgits"

In a few moments, I am back home in front of my door. I do not have the key with me. It is probably inside the house. I try to unlock it using a digital code and after two failed attempts, I look into my wallet in which I have placed the code written on the back of my visiting card "1101770".I enter the code and opened the door. I walk inside to see that one of my oscar fish, Red Lutino is on the verge of death, dead flat on the gravel. While my albino is waiting for me happily waving itself at the same time hungry for some worms. I rush to the food box and pick some live worms and pellets and drop them into the water. My albino feeds on it rejoicing the food while my red lutino still lies at the bottom. I feel heartbroken at the sight. If I did not make it today, my fish would die in a week. I grab the red lutino from the water touching it and placing some pellets into its mouth. It swims gradually and again sits at the bottom of the aquarium.

I walk towards my cupboard pick up my 35mm stills camera, a Yashica electro 35 and clean it. I pick a roll of Kodak film and load it into it. I feel good doing it since it has been quite a while since I touched it. I also pick my 300mm wildlife lens with the 2x extender and clean it. I need to shoot again some pictures I decide. I walk towards the kitchen and smell something foul. Some dishes are still lying there unwashed. I grab a mask and finish cleaning them. Someone grabs me from behind. As I try to turn, the person places their hands on my eyes. I believe it is a woman since I can feel those fingers which are slim and tender. I try to turn back, but she also moves behind me, I cannot see her. I walk into the hall.

"What took you so long dear?" asks Nila as she comes in front of me.

"Well you create all mess, fuck my mind and expect me to live in peace, don't you,"I ask in a frenzied burst of anger.

"What did I do?"

"You were hanging dead in this house the other day when I came here,"I say.

"I was just testing your guts," Nila says.

"Can you imagine how it feels?"I ask.

"Well you did imagine, already didn't you, how did you feel?"Nila asks.

"Can you please leave me and get out of my life?"

"Well I know you would say that you are fond of kissing someone lately, so you do hate me, cheat on me,"Nila says.

"Kiss someone? Are you out of your mind?"I say.

"Yes you did."

"Why would I? Do you think you gave my mind its freedom to do that? You did not,"I say.

"Yes, that is the only thing I possess because you never gave your heart to me, it is only the mind I can take over."

"Not so long," I say.

"I know you are trying to occupy in that photography work of yours, I do not mind as long as it gives me space but it makes you independent and makes me ignore you, I cannot accept that,"Nila says.

I push her aside and walk into the hall to see my Yashica dropped into the aquarium.

"You are crazy and nuts,"I shout at Nila

"Am I? So are you"

"What made you do this?"

"You try to keep your mind with you I don't bother, give me your heart or I will have to take your mind with me so hard that you cease to exist all by yourself."

"You have such sadistic pleasure in torture," I say.
"Well, you still do not understand how much I love you, do you? I am stuck in this mess not willing to give up just for you, do you realize how many times I saved you from wily occurrences of this nasty world? You would have been long dead. Just that you wanted to live here I am rescuing you from your ill mind which can hardly remember anything,"Nila says.
"It is you who made it like that, you barged into it so hard that it ceased to work on its own,"I say.
"You no longer deserve me,"Nila says.
"Either way, I am good, please leave me,"I say.
"I would if you have loved me from your heart," Nila says.
"After all that you did to my mind, do you ever imagine I would love you again from the bottom of my heart? No, I will not,"I say.
"Again? What a beautiful lie. You never did."
"You might be good at hovering over my mind but even if I truly love you with my heart, I am quite sure you can never get a hold of it. You have turned so cold that you cannot get even a tinge of my love or feelings from my heart."
"Let us test it out then, why don't you love me from your heart," Nila says.
"Just go away," I shout at her.

There is dead silence for the next two minutes and after a moment I hear the glass of my aquarium broken as if a stone is thrown at it from a distance. All the water floods onto the floor. My Red Lutino still stays at the bottom of the aquarium on the stand. While my albino afloat earlier drops onto the floor popping like ping pong. I go to my bathroom fetch a bucket, filled it with as much water as I could in few seconds, I quickly grab both the fish and place them into the water. I am tired. I should have probably stayed at the hospital. I see the fish trying to jump out of the water from the bucket. I realize that I have turned on my heater earlier so the water would have been hot, I grasp both the fish again and place them into another bucket filling some cold water into it. I am out of mind with all these encounters with Nila. I see the fish popping their gills in and out hard now, relieved from the trauma they just had.

I look at the broken glass sitting on the chair. I could see the reflection of two pale brown eyes staring hard at me. Bang Bang, followed by the sound of a lever cocking the film to advance further. I am looking straight into the eye of the tiger with translucent pale brown eyes.

"The tiger looked at me Daddy," He screams.

"It sure did my son, for you are as brave as a Tiger," Boy's Dad says.

"I took a picture of it Dad,"The boy says.

"You know how to use that Yashica, Son?"He asks.

"Yes I do,"He says.

"But I never thought you knew how to use it, how did you learn it?"He asks.

"I wasted a roll, then I brought a new 35 mm roll with my money,"He says.

"Your money? You are just 7 years where you got that money."

"Grandpa gave it to me while leaving."

"Alright so how do you know that you snapped the picture correctly?"

"You see this glass."

"The Rangefinder"

"Yes the Rangefinder has two lights inside which indicate the exposure, Red is over and Yellow is underexposed. If either light doesn't glow the exposure is correct."I say.

"Good," He said.

"This ring here is the aperture, as I turn it I can set it to whatever I want and the camera sets the shutter speed for me."

"So the camera says your shutter speed is fast or slow?"

"Yeah, the exposure gets correct only if the shutter speed is right which is correct only we choose the right aperture based on light conditions and just on how we need the picture."

"How did you get all this info?"

"I read the manual for every lost picture in the roll until the lights stopped glowing indicating the right exposure."

His father pats his hand on the Boy's head. The Boy is anxiously waiting for the picture of the tiger he just took. He will have to snap another 15 pictures until he finishes the roll. For now, he places his camera strap on his shoulder and walks along with his dad.

I am following the kid curious to know what picture he is going to take next. Everyone walks towards the giraffe next. Fathers are taking pictures of the giraffe while the mothers are posing with their kids. Most of them are using an automatic plastic lens camera or a disposable camera which loads a 35mm roll. While everyone is posing with the giraffe, the boy did not shoot the giraffe but actually took pictures of the family while they talk to each other. Such a strange kid with a wonderful perspective on life. But his fortune ended on the same day while during the elephant show in the zoo, he accidentally fell from the steel boundary and fell off to the ground and lost his life right there. Some people who hasn't noticed it yet were cheering the elephants while I was stuck with a blow to my head, shocked at what just happened. The boy was dead right there due to the fall on his head. The father from above cried for a while, fell unconscious and fell into the same ground where the boy fell but he did not die then. I rushed towards him, and along with the help of a few other volunteers, we admitted him to King George Hospital in Visakhapatnam. I was doing my graduation at that time over there. We waited for more than four hours. Some of the volunteers left. The last one left, handed over the belongings a blue bag of the kid and his Yashica camera. I waited for a few more hours then their relatives arrived. Seems the boy has no mother. The brother of the man in the hospital came rushing. They belonged to a middle-class family. In an hour the man was proclaimed to be in a state of coma.

On that day I was sitting outside the hospital for a very long time, and I slept there eventually. When I woke up everyone left except for the father inside the hospital. I collected the things of the boy and the camera and went to the duty doctor and asked him to pass them on to the family. He refused to take it and told me to come over the next day and pass it on. I opened the bag of the boy it had some rice in a box and biscuits. I decided to sleep there for the night as my bus pass would require me to pay if travelling after college hours and I did not have much money so I decided to save. The next day, I noticed the brother of the man sitting beside me under the tree where I slept.

"Hello Sir,"I said,he does not reply.

"How is your brother?"I ask.

"Thanks, Boy," He says.

"I did nothing," I say.

"Neither did we,"He says with his eyes red and throat bloated stuck with grief.

"How is your brother?" I ask again he does not reply.

"I hope he will recover soon Sir,"I say.

"I am killing him," he says stuck in deep thought.
"Why would you kill him?"I ask shocked
"If I had money, I can see my brother for a little longer but he is no longer the same mighty elder who does anything for his family. I cannot see him like that. Our son died. He can never be the same man."
I speak nothing.
"The doctor says there is no medical advancement over here to treat him, all they can do is sustain him in his coma state for a bit longer but that requires a lot of money for every passing day. They want me to decide in six hours. I did not speak anything over there. I know I cannot say anything. When God took the decision, there is nothing I can decide or say."
"Please take this Sir, their belongings" I take the blue bag and the camera and give them to him.
I also give him five thousand rupees from my pocket I had to pay for my tuition fees. He refuses to take anything.
"Son what do you do,"He asks me.
"I study here,"I say.
"You have done a lot for us, please go and take a rest. Now the situation is in the hands of God, we are just playing our roles."
I walk silently from there I do not know if I have to say a formal goodbye either. So I just started walking away.
"Son wait!"He keeps calling me in my direction
"Did you see my nephew before the fall? Was he happy?"He asks.
"Yes Sir, he was very happy. He took a picture of the tiger some time back and he was very delighted. His father was proud of him. I think it was one of their best days if not for what has happened."
He does not say a word. He pats my shoulder waits for a

while and says "Thanks Beta."
He throws the camera into the dustbin beside us. After that, he walked away back into the hospital. I did not understand why he threw the camera which is the one last thing that the boy was fond of, maybe he considered it a bad omen. I walked away from there a few yards and noticed a cat with pale brown eyes crossing my way. It did remind me of the tiger of which the boy took a picture. I ran to the dustbin and collected the camera. After a few days, I gave the role for processing and the picture of the Tiger turned out magnificent, capturing the vivid coat of the feline staring straight at the boy. The picture of the tiger is now hanging in my hall reflecting onto the broken glass. The man was put to death a month later as the family could not afford the treatment and there was no sign of progress post-treatment told the hospital staff later on. That moment was gone, but the impact and pain still remain every moment I stare at the picture.

I stare at the broken glass again retrieving my thoughts from the reflection to the present. Nila's malevolence is challenging me every day. Why is she so naive? Is that love? Would someone hurt a person when they love? Can love lead to possession? Or possession is altogether a different evil warding off peace in love. I do not have these answers, so I am stuck here with my mind offered to be fed by the devil in Nila. I open the pillbox and take some for sleep. I take a slight overdose. However, I am still awake. There is an old newspaper lying on the floor wet from the water on the floor. I remove it, fold it into a ball and pop it into the bin. I come back to recline on the chair. At that instant, something flashes in my mind. I go back to the bin and open the paper spread across the aquarium stand. It is a picture of the Berjaya Times Square. I have been there I recollect.

Tevy and I went there. Where is the watch? Where did I place it? I rush to the door and see the city chain plastic bag on the shoe rack but no watch in it. A rush of thoughts floods my mind as I tend to get dizzy. We had dinner. I also gifted her a watch. I drove along the beach with her. I kissed her. How did I forget all this? How has my mind selectively erased this till now? The pills I took for sleep had grasped my mind inducing a state of mild coma to it. My mind is in the grasp of the pills now, which could be the only reason I was able to hone these memories. I kissed her. We waved goodbye at the lift. She placed the watch on my hand. I kept it somewhere in the house. Tevy had loved me. We had entered into a relationship. How foolish am I? I forgot all this and did not talk to her these days. In my mind, I walk steadfastly to the door while physically I am sleeping on my bed now not knowing when I would wake up.

CHAPTER FOUR

1970 Khmer Republic (Cambodia)

Narrator: Heng Chann

I am walking over the stars stamping each one with my foot more hardly than you can fathom. I am jumping from one star to the other. The darkness between the jumps sends a shrill in my veins. Death is so wonderful. You are not confined to the shell anymore. It is like a cold water bath. The first pour of water seems colder yet gradually you tend to feel it normal. Death is frightening to see and experience as it happens, once it occurred you are more relieved than ever. The joy of meandering the planets, stars and galaxies is unparalleled. Would a bird ever choose to cut off its wings when it is alive? It will if it never knew how to fly. Now I know how to fly. The wings are more precious to me now than the rest of the bird. Do you prefer the body or the soul? A Body needs a soul to remain alive for its existence, but a soul does not need a body. I no longer need my body for I shall have my soul forever. Enlightenment with physical existence to a human is the most pathetic form of existence. It is similar to a state where you know you have the wings to fly, you knew about the flight but you cannot fly since your body is weighing you down. You are anchored to your daily mundane. You can let go of your ego, but you cannot let go of your needs. You have hunger, sleep and fear to tend to, which weigh you down. Death cuts off the chains holding you down. Even a helium balloon is confined to the atmospheric pressure which makes it float but after a certain point, it cannot take the pressure anymore and bursts. That burst is death. People see that the balloon is gone, and children cry at that spectacle but the truth is the balloon just got bigger, so big that you cannot measure staying in your finite body.

"Brother!!" cries Kala followed by four slap to me.

"Do not push me, Do not, stay away from her,"I mumble in dizziness dangling between my state of death and reality.

"Open your eyes, brother,"Says Kala.

"I wish I could but they burnt my body,"I say.

For another fifteen minutes or so there was silence.

"Get up! Wake up at once!"cries someone of a voice of an old woman which I probably heard before, followed by another three slaps on my right cheek and a flash of someone spraying water on my face hard.

I wake up to see the Yiey, Som Peou in front of me. This old lady is possibly treating me now. I look at my hands and legs everything is covered in ground leaf extracts. I am still not sure what is just happening to me. This old lady was selling some shady stuff the other day, and she was slightly rude to me in the past. She refused to talk to me earlier but now she is tending to me. What happened to me? Was I not supposed to be dead by now? Who would have saved me? Is my body intact? Many thoughts seem to bother me. More than all being treated by this old witch bothers me a lot.

"Wake up boy. I cannot sit here for you all day long" Shouts Yiey.

"Please," Says Kala to Yiey with folded hands to soften a bit towards me.

"Why is this old witch here?"I ask.

"Mind your words. This is our house," says the granddaughter of Yiey angry with a furrowing face.

"Please ignore him, Champa," says Kala to the granddaughter of Yiey

Finally, I got to know her name, knowing that I am in the house of Champa I try to control my aggression towards Yiey.

"Brother how are you feeling now, we were very worried for you?Kala says.

"Sorry," I say.

"Ridiculous" cries Champa in despise.

At this point, I would look if Sorya was around but I do not find him anywhere. I am also a bit worried that he spoke about the argument we had with Kala.

"What made you so desperate to kill yourself, brother? You may not be my real brother but you are the only one I considered as my blood brother, you should have told me about your problem," says Kala in a mix of tones from loud to soft and with a tinge of sadness as she softened the tone.

I say nothing. My silence is much better than the explanation I feel.

"You have cut your wrist with a knife and fell unconscious, there was no way you could have survived with such an injury,"Champa says with no feelings whatsoever on her face.

I feel slightly better as this is the first time she gave me a neutral expression usually it was a frown or despise.

"Thanks, Yiey," I say.
"Huh," She says,
"Yiey had ground all kinds of herbs to slacken your blood loss, Champa was attending to you all the while to keep your fever under control," Kala says.
"I am grateful to you Yiey and Champa,"I say trying unsuccessfully to fold my hands
"Stop! do not move your hand."cries, Champa.
I revert to my posture.
"If Kala had brought you here any late you would have been six feet under the ground by now," says Champa
"I wanted to die at that point but now after all that you have done, I do not feel alone anymore. Even my sister was taken away, but you are here for me, saved me."I say
"Relax brother you need rest," Kala says.
All the while one thought wanders my mind where is Sorya? I do not have an answer now, but I am not curious to know either after all that exchange of words between us.
I try to get up from the cot and put my legs on the ground.
"Stop it fool" shouts Yiey
"You who told me to get up and leave from here as you are old and cannot wait for me all day" I reply to Yiey controlling the urge to lash out at her.
"Fool," she says again.
Furiously my face turns red.
"She wants you to sit and take the medication she prepared out of herbs, she needed you to wake up not to leave,"Kala says.
I remain silent. For the next couple of hours, it would be better if I neither judge Yiey nor Champa I decide. I drink the greenish-brown liquid which tasted like seaweed.
"Sleep," Yiey says.
I relax back onto the bed and try to sleep again. I feel

good that I finally had someone for me. I knew Kala as a shrewd young woman who calls me brother but never knew how much she cared for me. I imagine the face of Champa before I can get into the clutches of slumber. Somehow I feel at home. My dream has come true partially. I am in the same house as Champa. I recollect what I have seen. When I was awake I was surrounded by stone pillars holding the tiled roof. The roof extends over from the rooms to the corridor surrounding the uncovered centre of the house where I lay sleeping. The house is quite big though the last time when Sorya and I came to meet Yiey all we could see was the humble entrance which has nothing but a square hole in the wall mounting a platform on which Yiey sits and sells stuff from the city. Practically there is no entrance to the house apart from the platform. The grandeur of the house is only visible after the rabbit hole or the entrance is crossed. It was a wise architecture for someone who wanted a modest living, concealing from the crowds. I start to think of my hut for a while and my oxen. I untied them when I left the place so I hope they are alive and eating grass elsewhere. I am a bit worried if they left forever, I do have bondage with them. I try to nullify my thoughts, the more I think I tend to get worried and cannot take a rest. At this point, I do not feel any pain in my body. My left-hand wrist is completely numb, and I am not sure about what was done to it. It was bandaged when I saw it earlier and I try not to think about it as I know it would look bloody from the wound made by slicing with the knife. I am still not sure how Kala discovered me in my hut and why Sorya was not here. These thoughts never cease to ease my mind. I let them pass over with no answers until a point where I am drained and devoid of anything else in my skull.

An urge to piss is not letting me rest any further. I see the familiar sky above me is quite dark now as I try to get up from the cot. I am surrounded by rooms in a circle around me a few metres radii from me. I am not sure how to get to the entrance and go out to urinate. I walk stealthily to one of the rooms. I just could not believe it is night already, only a few hours back I have seen morning light when I spoke to Kala. She would have left for her home now. I am left alone with the witch and the beauty. I hope I can find the witch before Champa finds me. I am shy to tell Champa that my bladder is swollen. The more I try to solve the maze of doors the more anxiety dawns on me leading to the urge to piss immediately. I bang on one of the doors.

"What is it?"Champa opens the door, her eyes gleaming in the moonlight, her hair all loose, she is wearing a white cotton robe which is lit like the moon and the light reflects on her face. My urge to urinate froze upon seeing her spellbound, and I was out of words for some time.

"I was looking for the exit," I say.

"You want to go home?"She says frowning at me.

I do not know what to reply, I stay silent.

"You seem to be more like a fool like Yiey said, you need to be given some medication and monitored for a while however it is up to you. Next time keep your knives away, we cannot wake up late at night due to your whimsical ideas about death" She says.

"I just need to tend to my nature call,"I say.

"Oh," She says and walks inside her room to get a bunch of keys. She walks towards her main door. I notice as she walks that the robe is wrapping her perfectly and her figure is like a vase so arousing. She is much more attractive than the dream I had with her in my hut.

"Come over," she whispers at me and points to the entrance indicating to go out and tend to the call.

I walk outside the hut, and as I do I recollect the same road at which we spoke to Yiey on the first day we met her. I walk to the spot where I was standing in isolation when Yiey was talking to Sorya. At midnight in the beautiful moonlight, the plants are vibrant like large diamonds. I curse them with the water jet from my penis shooting at whatever I wanted. The feeling that I am still alive in my village with vegetation makes me happy, especially since being in the same house as Champa is like God heard me after all. I come back to see Champa reclining over the entrance door in a sleepy state waiting for me. I knock on the door to let her know I am back, and I walk silently inside. Champa follows me. I walk straight onto the bed at the centre of the circular corridor surrounding the rooms. As I recline on the bed, I look at Champa with her hands on either door just about to close them, I smile at her. She closes the door with a dull thud and a blank expression on her face.

In an hour a slight drizzle occurs, and I pick up my cot along with the bedsheet and place it in the corridor. I close my eyes again then a jet of water pours upon my face disrupting my attempts to sleep again. This night seems long. I look at the door closed in my face earlier and I know I would be pushing the edge of my limits if I seek help from Champa again. Slowly the rain starts to pour harder, and I am half-drenched by now. I hear the creaking sound of the angry doors again, not closing but opening.

"Are you a kid?" cries Champa at me

"I was about to.."I try to finish but am interrupted by her.

"Can't you speak up for yourself?"She says.

"I thought you would be sleeping."

"Get inside, should I invite you again, you are drenching in the rain"

With that approval, I walk inside but I am a bit hesitant now. Though I was helped by the witch and this devil, as it so seems to me now with her persistent frustration towards me. I feel like going home.

"Take off your clothes," She says.

"What!"I say shocked.

"You would get sick again, take off,"She says.

I remove my clothing and place it on the wooden log as pointed to me by Champa. I still have my pants on.

"Remove that also," She says looking away from me.

"Done," I say as I stripped down to my inner loincloth.

"Let me get you some clothes," She says.

She walks inside the house pushing a wooden door with iron mesh outward and walks into rooms farther inside which I can only vaguely see in the darkness.

Fifteen minutes pass by and there is no trace of her. I walk towards the door and do not see her anywhere nearby. I retract to the point I started from and feeling shy, I sit on the bed aside. I wait for another hour and there is no trace of her. My loincloth is almost dry now, and my penis is fully erect due to the cold atmosphere. I sit on the bed so that at any moment Champa comes in she would not see me with an erection as I feel it would be very embarrassing. After 30 minutes, I decided that she would have probably slept in one of her rooms and so I decide to block the door with a wooden stool in the room and sleep. I walk towards the door, and Champa suddenly comes from the other end and we bash into each other.

"I am sorry," I say staring into her beautiful eyes. With her body against the moonlight coming from the door opposite to me, I could see her nipples protruding out of her breasts.

I am having a full erection, and she glances at it, involuntarily action I suppose. She advances further as I step back. My heart is racing like a horse now. She stares at my naked body. Place her hand on my body with mixed feelings pushing me back a little. She pushed me back harder now but did not remove her hand or glance away from me. With her hand still on my body, I caress one of her breasts. As I do so she half closes her eyes, feeling the surge of passion rushing inside her. I place my other hand on her back and pull her towards me. She holds my penis and grabs it hard. We rush towards the bed and kiss passionately. I lift her nightwear and engage passionately with her but at the peak of our moment, she pushes me slightly not knowing if that is the right thing to do. I retrieve my penis and ejaculate into my hands folded at the tip of it, with some residue on the bed. I am not worried or upset about not finishing the pleasure within her. I am confused. So is she, as I can tell from her expression. She walks away speaking nothing but grabbing the bed sheet and folding it into a ball, from the bed. I am spellbound. The last few minutes maybe thirty or maybe an hour passed like a dream to me but it was not. I felt her in my hands. It was the best moment of my life though I am still confused about her feelings towards me. I spread my hands and legs apart and slept on the bed finally releasing all the tension from my mind over the years, despite my confusion about where my relationship with Champa is going to head. I put on the clothes which Champa had brought for me.

"Wake up" Yiey screams at me.

"Sorry,"I say as I crouch on my bed.

"Drink this," She gives me some liquid in a copper tumbler.

"Okay," I say and finish it in a gulp.

Yiey gives me a hard stare and leaves. The way she looks

at me I can only think of two possibilities, either in some weird way she knew I was intimate with Champa and the other would be my extra caution towards her which I usually don't.

"Sleep," she says and leaves the room.

Sleep is the last thing on my mind now. My mind is racing towards what lies ahead of me with Champa. As Yiey leaves the room I walk towards the corridor and see no one. Where is Champa? Where could she be now? Will she talk to me? Is she loving me or despising me? Many questions run through me. I hope I can get a reply today but I am not sure. The moment when we were together she held me so close that she possibly wanted me without a second thought but will that persist ever? I do not know. I go towards the wall near the entrance of the house. I look at the well wrapped with green slimy climbers. There is a narrow rock stair inside the well leading to the bottom. I peep into the well not sure if there is any water inside.

"You can bath in it,"Yiey says.

"I don't see water in there," I say.

"See again,"Yiey says and leaves the place.

I peep into the well again and see white reflections in the dark water. I retrieve the can hanging over the log running along the diameter of the well atop. I drop it into the well to fill the water in it. The rope runs till the end of the knot over the log with a dull thud. I retrieve it and see that it is empty. From then, every passing second intrigues me and makes me believe that Yiey is nothing lesser than a witch.

"GO inside the well,"Yiey's voice hovers over my back. I look back but she is not there. What kind of creepy place is this? I think. I am not going to stay any longer over here I decide.

"GO inside and take a bath,"Yiey says, this time she is standing at the source of the sound at my back.

I am scared. Probably I did not notice her earlier but as I think I recollect she was not standing there earlier. I walk gradually into the well tracing each step as I place my foot down. Now I am more worried about what happened yesterday. Did the witch know everything? Is this her way of sorcery to kill me? I feel a sense of fear that someone is actually behind me as I go down the stairs. I dare not look back. After a few rounds of circumventing the well, I can longer see any light. I perceive each step of mine to go downward by placing my foot and tracing the next move. I look upward and there is no light at all. It feels like I am in a dungeon now. I cannot see the opening of the well. I place my foot to trace and see there is no next step either. I want to go back. The sense of fear now hits me harder than before. I sit on the step and try to trace back by placing my hand on the earlier step, and I do not feel it either. All I have now is the step on which I am sitting nothing further or backwards. There is no light only darkness.

"Jump," says Yieys voice hovering over my ears but I do not see her anywhere.

"Jump," says the voice again

I should have the house yesterday night left when I went outside for urination, I regret it now. I knew in many instances that this old witch is not an ordinary woman. Her eyes do not seem like that of any mortal person. There is a deep mystery in her eyes. They change colour and shape every time I observe her. The first day I met her they were ruby red with brown accents. Later when she rescued me with her medication and when Kala was beside they were like turquoise blue. In the room today, her pupil was a light tint of green. Now her eyes are pitch black. It was as if her eyeballs were removed completely. All the minute details I ignored about her seemed to creep into my mind now and there is nothing good about it.

"Jump," says Yiey's voice again.

I can no longer take this. I need to decide now. I am prepared to die but not to suffer. What if the old witch makes me suffer instead?

"Jump, Jump, Jump,"repeats the voice over and over

I have no option if this is my destiny so be it. I do not have to close my eyes even if I jump as right now it is dark and I do not see anything. I try to make the jump but again I held back for a moment just to relish that moment I had with Champa as I am anyways going to die, I suppose. I recollect the moments with Champa but this time I do not have an erection. My feelings towards my fate seem to suppress the passion in my body. All I could recollect are mere images. Images of Kala at her house, Sorya at the field, my father in the house and my mother frowning at me, my baby sister who always looked at me strangely. My world is small, it probably does not matter even if it ceases to exist at this very moment. I know apart from Kala no one is going to bother about my whereabouts. Maybe Sorya would shed a tear, but I am not sure.

I plunge myself into the darkness. I am floating in the air moving towards the bottom of the well. I do not feel any sense of gravity. All I could feel is a rush of air passing through the gaps in my fingers and at the tip of the hair on my head. In an instance, I am forced into a hard plunge downward. This is the end. The speed at which I descend is so fast that I can feel the burns on my body. The tips of my hands start to burn. My hair is lit by golden fire. I am moving faster than the shooting stars I see at night. My body is ripping itself apart as I am pulled down. My nose could not sustain to resist any more, the incoming air jet ripped it and it just flew above me. My nose is gone, and my ears are chipped off. One of my feet got twisted and is ripped by the fierce air rushing towards me. In a few minutes, I lost everything. My body is gone, ripped, burnt and scattered. I only have my mind. I can see. I am not sure if my eyes are with me. I can only feel that I can see, there is no mirror to validate nor do I have my limbs to touch and feel if my eyes are where they were.

A mother is breastfeeding her child. The baby child looks bigger than a just-born but not as big as a kid either, he could be probably two years old. She runs her hand on his head. She kisses him on his forehead. She is weeping. She knows she is going to die soon, someone unknown disease is bothering her. The disease may or may not kill her, but death is certain, these are her last moments with her son. Someone is pounding on the wooden door of her hut. A group of people barge into her hut. They drag her by the hair onto the street. They pelt stones at her. She waves her hand to stop as they would hurt the child. The people do not stop, they are enraged. The mother holds the baby boy in her hands and runs as far as she can. The crowd mostly men, runs following her trying to snatch. She kicks a stone accidentally and falls to the ground. The angry mob are shouting at her. One of her breasts is still open for the baby to have milk. She never had the time to cover herself from the mad crowd running towards her. She prays to them to let her leave. The crowd continues to curse her. They ask her to die elsewhere and not in the city.

"Please leave me, spare me, don't kill my child," She says.

Two man talk to each other within the crowd. A lady interrupts them and comes out shouting to kill that child or the village will suffer the imminent spread of disease.

Gradually everyone agrees with the lady's opinion. In an instant, the clamouring crowd chases the mother and the pelting of stones continued. As the mother runs away from the crowd her attire is now dishevelled, pieces of cloth torn by the pelted stones and blotches of mud and sand picked from the ground, spread all over her hair, skin and cloak. While most of the crowd is chasing her, the rest is watching the incident amusingly with utmost curiosity. Some feel it is wrong to make the women suffer but all their help is limited to gossip with their neighbours and mere sympathy with no actions. With the crowd growing mad every minute, the sense of fear in the mother increases multifold. She is trembling involuntarily. Her heart is palpitating. She is sweating profoundly. It was a hot day and the tense atmosphere only added to the heat of the situation. Escaping the gripping hands of the crowd, the mother begins to run farther, crossing the fields. She runs so fast that all she could feel is the kid in her hand and the sweat on her brow dripping like a river and touching her nose as it does so. Her feet are numb, yet they are preset with running that much she knows. After a moment a hard stone hurling towards her hits on her head, and she collapses to the ground. The impact of the fall is so great that the sound awakens everyone in the neighbourhood to come out and see the spectacle. The child is knocked unconscious by the fall along with the mother. The stone-pelting continues until they reap every bit of life from the woman measured by the drop in her bodily moments. Within a few minutes, the mother lies unperturbedly by the kicks, stones or bashes by the crowd. Satisfied the crowd now continues their gossip and accolades each other for accomplishment. An old man in brown tattered rags, greedy eyes and clumsy hair walks towards the mother as the crowd is ready to walk away from her awaiting the old man to conclude.

"She is dead," says the old man. The crowd still looks at him expecting something more.

"The child is also dead," he says. In an instant, the crowd disperses like they never knew the dead mother and child until before and nothing of her is in their interests. They just walk away. The man in ragged clothes picks up the mother and the child and placed them into the rear of the cart brought by a young man looking similar to the old man, probably his son.

"Where shall we dump them?" says the son as he flogs the oxen driving the cart.

"We need to move quickly," says the old man to his son whose face is covered in the shade of the sun, only his silhouette is traceable against the sun.

After a few kilometres, the son repeats the question to his father.

"Where shall we bury them?"

"Lets us go home first," says the old man

"Home? Are you out of your mind? If you take these bodies home, we will be flogged to death like the fate of the woman"

"Go," says the old man triggering his son to flog the oxen again into a jerky start.

After a few yards as they pass by the river the old man interrupts.

"Drive the cart below this stone bridge."

The son veers his cart to head towards the entrance of the bridge but does not head into it but steers into the narrow mud path beside.

"Drink this," says the old man handing his son some rice wine

"Why?" says the son

"Drink it," he says again.

Confused the son gulps the drink down his throat. Though he did not intend to have it at that moment, the first sip made him savour another.

"Enough, we got work to do," says the old man as he grabs the small bottle casket from his son's hand.

His son begins to dig the ground under the bridge, the thought that someone would interfere is now distant in his mind. He surpassed his fears of society and started to dig faster. He walks towards the rear of the cart and picks the woman on her shoulder and places her gently into the pit dug by him. He walks again to the rear to pick up the child and place him beside the mother.

"Father! Are you crazy see what you have done,"cries the son loudly but is only heard by his father as there is no one nearby.

"I know,"Father says.

"What shall we do now? You knew this?"

"I did."

"Are you out of your mind?"

"I am perfectly sane."

"Who will take care of the baby."

"The same God whom you pray to every day,"

"How can I tell it to her?"

"You do not have to."

"What do you mean?"

"I will give this child to someone who needs."

"Who will take it, how did you pick the child after you knew that he is still alive."

"Your question has the answer. I picked up since he is still alive."

"He would have probably borne the disease into him from

his mother."

"He did not," says the old man

The old man picks up the child and places him in the pit hole in which the mother is laying.

"Are you crazy," cries the son

"Bury it," says the old man

"How can you bury the living child,"Son cries.

"How do you expect me to betray a living child then,"Father says,as he picks some sand and places the child into the pit.

"You are insane, stop it." Son cries as he jumps into the pit and picks up the baby.

"What will you do now?The old man says.

"I will raise him."

"Will your wife agree?"

"I am not married yet, it doesn't matter,"says the son

"It matters someday, says the old man in a soft tone as he jumps onto the rider's seat this time.

With unforeseen attention induced into his head, the son rocks the baby and gets into the rear.

They near their home, a hut covered by straw on a wood frame and mud walls. Two oxen laying plopped outside the hut looking at another two oxen on which the father and son are approaching home.

I am sitting on the steps. The revelation ripped me. I could trace steps ahead of me and behind me lining the well. I wanted to go ahead. I want the truth. I am no longer afraid of the darkness around me. I place my step downwards confidently without tracing it. Even if the next step meant death, I was ready to face it. I want the revelation more than my reality. As much as I want to see my biological mother, I was also repulsive to see her suffering during her last moments. I take another step further and plunge again into the depth of the well. A big splash of dark water is picked by my ears. I am now in the water seen earlier by me from the top. The water is so refreshing that it is washing the memories etched into my heart. My sense of purpose is lost. I am besotted with the water flowing all around me. I feel liberated spiralling in this water.

In a few minutes, I am standing beside the well.

"What are you staring at?fetch the water from the well using the bucket." Yiey says staring at me with ruby-red eyes.

"I already did, I just plunged into the river and knew everything, I was soaked in the dark water,"I say.

"Really," Yiey says looking at my chest

I look at my chest in response to the pointer from Yiey to notice that I am very dry with no hint of water anywhere. I also do not remember climbing the stairs up to the well.

"Thank you for pacifying me by showing me the truth from the past. I am grateful for what you have done,"I say.

"There is no truth or myth. Existence is a perception. You believe what you see, so you saw what you can believe."Yiey says.

I am walking past the corridor, and I see Champa. She is calm and more natural the way I had felt about her in my dreams.

"Sorry for"I say without knowing how to complete the sentence. Champa walks away without uttering a word which is quite unusual. She always responds to me like blazing guns. However, she is not frowning at me like she usually does. I do not have any clue why I am staying at this house. I do not want to go either not knowing what is crossing Champa's mind. Except for the bruise on my hand wrapped in a cloth fabric and some slimy leaves put into it by Yiey the rest of my body is fine.

"I am leaving,"I say to Yiey.
"Your wish,"Yiey says.
"I am very thankful to you and Champa," I say.
"Take good care, if you feel like dying come to me I can help without pain," Yiey says smiling at me. This is the first positive note from her since I met her. I did not even know that her facial muscles know how to smile.

I walk towards Champa's room but did not find her inside. I pick up my things and walk towards the entrance. I stand by the well for a few moments. I look at the water. It is always dark glistening with white streaks of light as it moves.

"Where are you going" Startled by the voice I look back at Champa talking to me
"Well it's time to leave,"I say.
"So you are done with the work you came for?"She says.
Puzzled, I do not know what to say.
"Did you eat something?"Champa asks.
"I am not very hungry," I say.
"Wait," She says as she treads into the house.
This is not the Champa I usually speak to, she is very serious, defensive, slightly abusive and never gives up on a discussion without an argument.
"Have this "She hands me two bananas.
"Thanks," I stay still holding the bananas in my hand.
"I hope you are not angry for the way I am with you since you came to this house,"She says.
"No that is perfectly alright, I am amused by your attitude towards me."
"Amused? So you never considered me seriously?"
"No, I did not mean that I liked"Kala walks in towards us before I can finish the sentence.
"Hello Brother, Hi Champa,"Kala says.

"Hello," we say.

Champa was a bit perturbed by the sudden appearance of Kala when she was about to hear something from me for which she was curious, I could figure this out from the slight blank expression on her face with a tinge of a frown.

"Where are you going, brother?"Kala asks, looking at me standing with my jute bag hung by my shoulder

"Home, I feel I am in good health so,"I say.

"Okay so it was your decision,"Kala says.

Champa shrugs at Kala

"Can he now leave Champa?" Kala asks.

"I do not know if he feels like leaving I cannot stop him, he is not a kid,"Champa says.

"What if he was a kid? What is your say"

"I would not send now," Champa says.

I look into Champa's eyes and can feel a tinge of lovingness for me to stay in her house. I am stuck in between at this point. I do want to stay with her, but I do not find any need for me to be apart from her either. I have surpassed the fears of death and do not have any curiosity to explore it nor do I have in finding who my parents are. The one thing that runs in mind now is Champa. I want to live with her.

"So what is your say,"Kala asks.

"I have to take care of my oxen and the hut," I say.

"The oxen who you have left and the hut which you decided never to return to? You now want them, brother? I am glad that you want"Kala says.

"Yes what I did was wrong, I did realize it only after I came here," I say,

"Glad to hear that brother,"Kala says.

"It is time to leave, "I say.

"Please come to my home brother, you, don't have to stay alone in that house,"Kala says.

"I need some solitude Kala and do not worry I will be fine. I just need some time to introspect and get into my regular course of life,"I say.

I walk towards the entrance while Champa and Kala follow me. I am surprised or shocked? I cannot relate at this point, but I see Sorya sitting and waiting on a cart outside. Probably he has come over to drop his wife off and pick her up when she leaves again. The fact that he is resourceful for the recovery of my health, despite the dispute we had, made me happy. I am confused if to get onto the cart or walk along the road. I still have memories of what he spoke to me. I continue to walk on the mud road slightly confused about which way leads to my hut.

"Brother? Where are you going? Stepin to the cart "Kala says.

"I am sorry sister. I prefer to walk please do not misunderstand me, "I say.

"You arc not supposed to walk, especially this summer in the hot sun,"Champa says

"You hear that brother?"Kala says.

"This is not my cart. I borrowed it, if someone is unwilling can pay for it later," Sorya says

It has been a long time since I heard his voice. I feel reluctant to walk, especially in the blazing heat. If not for what Sorya had said I would have felt stupid for walking all along. I silently step inside the cart onto the right while Kala sits on the left side. Champa looks at me with her beautiful eyes like two moons overthrowing the dazzle of the sun to dust. I get down the cart again. Champa is looking serious about such a foolish move in front of Kala and her husband. I walk closer towards Champa.

"I am very grateful for making me live again. I do not know what to say further, as your mind is like the ocean to me. It seems very familiar at once and suddenly I cannot fathom how deep you think."

Champa says nothing.

Yiey is staring at us from the shop facing the road. I walk towards Yiey.

"I am very grateful for all the help you did, emotionally you made me more stable than rescuing me physically. Now I know why people seek your help" I say

"Whatever is in your mind should not what be happening, if you impose you will have to bear the consequences, do not stare at the stars," Yiey says.

I am having goosebumps. She is no ordinary woman. How did she know I was looking at the stars?

"Chum Reap Leah,"I say to Yiey bidding goodbye

I step onto the cart again taking one final glance at Champa while she is looking at me all the while.

The absurdity I created by stepping out of the cart and speaking to Champa is now nullified by my move to interact further with Yiey.

As we tread along the mud road in the cart, all of us are silent. Kala is silent as she is aware that anything she speaks could ignite a difference between us. Sorya seems to be enjoying riding the cart or maybe he is acting so. I sit here on the straw mat rocking back and forth on the uneven road. As we near my home I look at Kala.

"Please come, home brother,"Kala says, Sorya could have heard or may not which I am not sure.

"Later, I will come Sister for today I will have to go home and gather myself,"I say.

"As you wish," She says.

The cart comes to a stop at my hut indicating that Sorya overheard our conversation or it was his idea that I will go home.

"Thank you" I utter in a slightly louder voice so that Sorya can hear as I get down the cart. I put my hands into the pocket of my cloak to fetch some money.
"Brother!! Stop it" Kala says as she can figure out what I was trying to do.
"Sorry," I say retrieving my hand from the pocket and continuing walking towards my hut.

I see the three oxen still sitting there with their flesh reduced to the bones. They did not eat well as I supposed they would elsewhere. There are dried leaves scattered everywhere. The door of my hut is closed, I do not remember closing it. Probably Kala would have done it while taking me to Champa's place.

I walk inside my hut and feel instantly bored not knowing what to do. For once I go out and drive the three oxen towards some fields for fodder. While they chew, my mind wanders for the time lost since I last left my hut.

At about dawn, I reach home sitting in front of the hut. I did not cook anything. I am not hungry. I place my straw mat in front of the house and sit on it staring at the road. There is some waste concentration nearby and the fumes of that fire hit my nostrils causing an uneasy feeling. I walk towards my field hoping that the pungent fumes abate. On my way, I feel someone pelting stones at me. I increase my stride in complete shock as to why would someone do that. I could feel the stones randomly hit on my body and so I run. I kick myself into a stone accidentally and as I fall I understand that the memory of my mother carrying me while running had a profound impact on my mind. I began to weep. I thought I was liberated by the experience in the well but the murder of my mother and thoughts of those transgressors who tortured her is making me restless. The aftermath of the events unnerved me. The people be it my father or Sorya or whoever kept the truth away from me did it for the same reason. My anger towards Sorya is gradually settling like sediment in still water. I reach my fields and see that there was a new layer of ploughing done maybe by Sorya. I walk back home as the air is more clear.

"Hello brother," says Kala standing near my hut as I approach it.

"How are you?"I ask.

"I am fine, but how about you looks like you are wandering somewhere."

"Nothing I just went for a walk"

"I brought some food for you," says Kala.

"I had food"I lie to her.

"You did?"She asks.

"Yes"

"What did you cook?"

"Rice and Potatoe,"

"You finished it."

"Yes I did finish."

"I am standing here for the past hour. I know you did not cook, you left this place before dusk and you are back now, Why are you lying to me?"

"Sorry I did not mean to"

"Well now do not embarrass yourself and me by explaining it further, I can understand, "Kala says.

I take the food container from her which is four cylinder-shaped wood caskets.

"I will meet you again brother, have to get some spices for cooking from the shop,"Kala says.

"Alright, thank you for undergoing the trouble to get this food and especially waiting so long for me, "I say.

"Do not say that," Kala says as she walks away towards the street.

I have my supper which is quite delicious with spicy spinach and cabbage. There is also a desert accompanied made of sugar and ground coconut shaped into a ball could be an Indian dish. After a long time, I had a heavy meal. After an hour I walk towards Kala's house to hand back the container to her hoping she would be back home by now.

I knock on the door of their house but no response. I wait for a while and knock again to no avail. Finally, I decide to leave. As I turn my back against the door, I could hear grunting sounds.

"Kids" I shout to which the grunting noise increases "Sorya" I scream and the sound increases rapidly with a rumbling of a steel vessel on the ground.

"Oh no!! Sorya it is just you inside, wait to let me get in," I say, I use all my force to bash on the wooden door ahead of me held by the mud walls. There was a log placed horizontally at the centre of the door as a locking system. There is practically no way I would be able to get through the main door. I pull hard and remove some of the palm-thatched leaves on the roof of the hut reclined towards the front. I jump over the seven-feet hut and climb on top of it. I remove some of the dried palm leaves on top. Now the ground inside the hut is slightly visible, but I still cannot find Sorya. I barge into the house after three heavy jumps over the roof. I fall with a thud, and my left knee has a heavy impact due to my temerity.

A few feet away laid Sorya with his arm near his chest, fist bent like a drooping flower over the stem. His legs are stiff. His face is tight with lockjaw. Horrified by the scene I rush towards him in an instant with all my pain ignored at that moment.

"Sorya are you alright?"I ask though I know the answer that he is not. I pick him up not knowing what to do next.

I have never faced this situation in the past. Sorya could raise resting on me but his left leg and arm are not under his grasp. I can now see what Sorya had told me earlier. His suffering is humongous. I just could not imagine his situation if Kala was not home anytime soon. I release the log across the door and open it. I place him on the mud steps of his entrance to go and stop any vehicle going by. Just at that moment, Sorya grasps my shirt and waves his hand towards the right side of his house. I do not understand what he is trying to convey. Confused I walk towards that direction and see a cart with its head reclining to the ground and two oxen nearby grazing on the dry straw fed to them. I lock the cart to the oxen and get it near the steps and place Sorya at the rear. I flog the right ox and then they stride. It seems like the oxen are aware that we are undergoing an emergency. On the way, I could see Kala approaching me. She hasn't noticed me yet. I do not know how to tell her about this situation. Sorya did not want Kala to be aware of all this. I am not sure where the kids of Kala are probably they were playing somewhere. I did not lock the house, so kids can get inside. But what about Kala? Sorya is sleeping at the rear, and I cannot wake him up now to debate and conclude, I do not have much time to do that. If I stop at Kala, I am not sure what would be the consequence of our already broken friendship. I have two options, move fast and hide from Kala or stop and inform her. By the speed at which the cart is driven, I only have a few seconds to decide.

CHAPTER FIVE

2016 MALAYSIA

Narrator: Arka

Did you ever see a shark with fins cut and bearing the head of a human? I did. Do you think it is Nila? You may, I did. But we are wrong. Nila is not the shark. I am the shark. Fins severed, heading towards the bottom of the ocean heading towards a slow death. In reality, a very slow death determined by Nila, not by me.

I wake up and stare at the clock indicating 5 AM. I close my eyes and indulge in sleep again. The shark and the couple kissing on the beach revisit my thoughts. Am I the shark or the guy kissing Tevy on the beach, only time can decide? I sleep for an indefinite time in space and wake up with my eyes, half-opened.To my surprise, the time is still 5 AM. Maintenance, nothing runs by itself. I recline back a little revealing a cube-shaped box with a leather texture as I move near to it I could see Titus embossed on it. I open the box to see hands at 11 AM on the watch. It is an automatic watch and is not wound for a couple of days I am not sure if that time is accurate either. Though the second's hand is still moving. Tevy comes into my mind as I looked at the watch. I dress up, have a bath, and look at the Oscars in the cold bucket.

"Don't worry guys I will find a home for you,"I say thinking that I will have to splurge some money for a comfortable one to handle the filtration process by itself and an automated feeder in case I am away from home again. A Smidgen of my mind is thinking about Tevy. I will have to talk to her. With a streak of sunlight shimmying from my window, I rejoice at that moment. I stand in the hot shower for a while and cleanse my body. After I dress up in a dark levis tee and ice blue jeans, I fetch the Titus watch and strap it across my wrist, it is a dress watch but there is nothing wrong in layering with some contemporary clothing, I convince myself. I fetch my Burgman keys and walk towards the elevator just to realize I do not know where Tevy is staying. I press the ground button and sit in the common area for a while on what should be my next move. I check with the building management, but they are not aware of any resident by the name of Tevy. She is probably staying as a paying guest which the management is not tracking.

I start my Burgman scooter and drive to Sea World aquarium shop 10 miles away from my house. As I reach, I notice an old tin-roofed warehouse. It has been here for probably a couple of years now. There is nothing fancy about the warehouse. It is surrounded by a lot of green random plants and grass. However, inside the warehouse lies all the fantasy. There were big tanks with domestic and wild species of fish. An exotic range of cichlids, varieties of Arowana and unique breeds are inside. There is an exquisite range of glass tanks with modular lights rendering light to reveal more specific details of the water tank. I was immensely impressed by the collection. There were an elephant nose, a jewel cichlid and a pufferfish. I finally managed to stay focused and purchase a tank. It was a

4-feet tank, and I would be provided with delivery for an additional 70 ringgits. A man in his forties with a wrinkled face and a white long beard asked for my phone number to call me before delivery. I replied saying I do not have a phone with me. He subtly sighed indicating that I am naive. I made the payment without any botheration about how they would consider me. Delivery is to be expected in the next 4 hours. I assured him that I would be at home by then. He did a thumb up at my reply. I start my scooter trying to comprehend where Arka would have been now. She hasn't left even a note at my door. I drive to a nearby food court and order banana Prata and have some coffee. While I sip my coffee, I notice a Maxis telco outlet right opposite me with a discount on the mobile handset if paired with a postpaid sim. I finish my coffee and stare at their outlet with a puzzled stare. A young lady wrapped in her long skirt outfit like luggage wrapped in polythene at the airport handed me the catalogue of phone models. After going through the pricing, I decide to get the Samsung Note 7 with unlimited data. The lady takes my details and informs me that I would receive my bill starting from the first of the next month for a year which would be the duration of my mobile contract. My mobile number is indicated on a sticker which is on top of the sim card sleeve. The lady informs me that she will give me a call to check, post my connection is activated. I place the phone in my jeans pocket and the rest of the papers and the box in the storage of my scooter. It is already more than two hours since I came from my fish tank warehouse. I head towards home with a slight feeling of accomplishment and disgust that I have purchased a phone. I park my scooter in the basement parking when I see the silhouette of someone standing right in front of me blocking my way. I take a turn to the right avoiding the person and park. I turn back to notice Tevy staring at me.

"I was at the hospital I was sick" I try to explain to Tevy. She is silent. With the loudest possible sound, the phone in my pocket begins to ring and vibrate. The vibration is so loud that it overpowered the ringtone as well. I told Tevy I never had a phone, this was a very awkward moment when I have to disclose that I just brought the mobile. Before I say anything Tevy walks out of the place without uttering a word. I rush towards the escalator since if I miss this moment it will be very hard to find out which floor and unit she is staying at but by then she closes the doors and the lift moves up. I check where the escalator stops. I hope someone does not use the lift before Tevy. I notice four and climb four floors and no sign of the elevator. I gasp at the fifth and a sixth. I could see it stopped. I stride to the right to see no sign of her and then towards the lift and the right covering a semi-circle to notice footwear outside the door similar to women of her age. I press the bell of the door after some thought.

"What do you want?" uttered a wrinkle-faced old woman with a frown on her face like that of a bulldog.

"I am looking for Tevy,"I say.

"What Tevy?" the old woman says.

"You have a granddaughter," I ask.

"Why do you ask?".

"Well I am not sure if I am at the right house," I say.

"He is looking for me Nanny," says Tevy from the back of my head

I stare at her with joy since I no longer need to bait this old woman.

"Are you sure? He seems crazy, stay away from him"the wrinkled mouth says.

Tevy chuckles at her and walks past me for another two units on the left and half closes the door. I walk after her not very sure if that is an invitation for me to walk in. The half-closed door is an indication that I should possibly walk out without much say. I knock on the door gently. Tevy walks over and opens the door. As I walk inside, I could see a cosy apartment decorated with live plants in almost every corner of the house. At my knees there is a leather sofa. I sit on the edge of it. I am sure Tevy is irked by my presence on her sofa sitting right in front of her. We remain silent for a minute. My phone rang again.

"Are you interested in a personal loan?"The caller says.

"No, I am not. Thanks,"I say as I disconnect the call.

Tevy grabs my phone rudely from my hand, dials in some number and then distantly I could hear a faint ringtone. She walks towards the direction of the ringtone placing my phone on the glass tea set in front of me. I am perturbed by her actions and not quite sure of what I should be doing next. After a minute, I recline myself on the sofa. A message beeps on my phone sending the tremor of the vibration to a pencil placed on the glass. I pick up the phone to see a message from an unknown number.

"Yes," says the text message.

"What is your problem" arrives another text almost instantly.

"Who is this?"I reply.

Tevy walks into the hall where I am sitting and displays her phone facing me in a flat hand indicating that it is she who is sending the message.

"I am sick, so I went to the hospital,"I reply.

"You went to the hospital and got a phone?"

"I got a phone, so I can avoid this situation in future, hereafter I can call you," I reply.

For the next fifteen minutes, there is utter silence in the home. Tevy comes over with two coffee mugs in her hand and hands over one of them to me. I grasp it.

"Thank you," I say, she nods in response.

I am stifled by her presence not knowing how to start a real tete-a-tete conversation.

"Oh No!" I utter before looking at the clock.

"You have to leave now is it," She asks.

"Yes I ordered a fish tank. They may deliver in the next hour," I say.

"Here you go, I hope you re-appear next month at least or probably leave it to my imagination on your rendezvous."She says.

"No, it is just that the delivery guys could reach me anytime and I do not have a phone."

"Really!"

"I mean I did not have a phone when I purchased the tank. I got the phone on my way from there."

Silence follows for the next few minutes. I made a microscopic movement to the resting hand on the sofa.

"You can leave if you want," She says.

"Leave!"I say.

"Yes you can leave if you have to for whatever concerns you have lined up at your door," She says.

"Only the tank, I still got time, an hour. I was alarmed if I missed the schedule before I noticed the clock. There is no rush now."

"So what did you buy?"She asks.

"Phone?"I ask.

"No," She says.

"Oh Alright, I just got the tank for the fish, nothing else"

"What happened to the one in which they already are,"She says.

"That shattered yesterday."

"So you were in your unit yesterday?"She asks.

"Yes, I am,"I say trying to cut the details as much as possible as it might seem like a cover-up if I give a hefty explanation.

"Did you think about me yesterday?" She asks,

"I did."

"I hope you did,"

"I was wondering about which floor you stay on, was pondering about you all day"

"So now you know."

"Ya and we are good."

"Good for what?"

"For whatever we seemed to be,"

"I am not going to indulge forth in your proposals further. I need some time to think."

"I am sorry," I say.

"So what's the reason you went to the hospital"

"Headachc"

"Anything serious?"

"No nothing, I am good"

"Do you get it often?"

"Sometimes"

"I am sorry," She says.

"Why," I ask.

"I should have asked enquired about your health earlier. Your sudden disappearance made me go bonkers."

"You have my number now. This shall not happen again."

"Shall we go?"

"Go?"I ask with a question mark face.

"We can go to your unit."

"I need to do some cleaning."

"That is alright. I can help you. We should sit there now since you get the fish tank delivered."

"I forgot about that."
"Let us go."

We enter our unit.

"There are some micro glass bits,"Tevy says.
"Is it?"
"Do you need glasses to read?"
"Yes I do,"
"That explains"
"I cleaned up the broken glass with a broomstick. Not sure about using the vacuum cleaning for this,"I say.
"You have duct tape? I also need a towel."
"Alright, Mademoiselle"

I pick up the stuff asked for and pass it on to her.

"Will this do?I ask.
"I also need a bucket of water."

In the next thirty minutes, the floor is clean. Tevy is a real workhorse. She has intricate skills in cleaning especially without missing the minute details.

The doorbell rings, and we walk over to the door. It is the delivery guys with the fish tank. They place the tank on the table as directed by me. I connect the canister filter and fix the led lights to the aquarium hood.

"I will place the fish in the water,"Tevy says.
"I bet you do. You deserve that ceremony launch," I say.

I direct her to the bucket where the two fish were kept. She picks up both the fish meticulously one after the other placing them into the tank.

"Isn't the tank supposed to run for a while without the fish?"
"Do not worry they are quite hardy?"I say.
"So were are risking aren't we?"
"If we leave the fish in the bucket for another week, they will die."

"Okay I get it."
"Let me cook something for you,"I say.
"That's alright. I am here to help you in the first place."
"Hold on, you did help a lot, let me make some pasta,"I say.
"I will have a bath and come back. My hands are slimy,"Tevy says.
"You can have a bath over here, while I cook if you do not mind,"I say.
"Alright then," She says.
I pass on the towel to her and walk into the kitchen to cook. Fifteen minutes passed, and I am waiting for her in the living room. She walks over in one of my shirts, pants missing.
"I am sorry, I turned the knob to the wrong side and got my clothes wet. Drenched I found your shirt nearby and wore it.
"That's alright," I say.
"Your trousers are too loose for my waist,"
I smile at her.
"Your pasta is ready"
"Looks yummy," She says as she places a fork full of it into her mouth.
"Delicious," She says.
"Thank you."
I try to avoid eye contact, but she looks so hot in my shirt. I stare at her bare legs.
As we finish the pasta, I carry the plates to the kitchen.
"Let me do it,"Tevy says.
"That's okay, you are my guest I say."
"So you kiss your guests," She asks.
"Ya I did to only one of them."
"So you remember but you seem to act like I am a stranger and avoided me after the moments we had at the beach."

"I am not avoiding you."

I step ahead, place my arm around her waist and draw her near me. I kiss her on her lips and as I do I caress one of her breasts with my hand. I grasp her so tight that the temperature raises between us in the warmth. We are fuming with passion. I notice no resistance. She likes probably this as much as I am. She kisses me on my chest as she unbuttons my shirt. I also unbutton her shirt revealing her naked body lit by the studio lights of the kitchen detailing every shape and its curvature to me. She closes her eyes as we hug each other. I ejaculate into her and then we kiss each other passionately. We conclude our lovemaking with more kisses. I place some coffee in the cups for both of us to retrieve from the pot at the coffee bean machine. Adding milk and sugar, I stir and pass it on to her. We sit in the living room staring at the window in silence. It could be we are retrospecting our actions. We have nothing to talk about regarding the past as our intimate session has concluded and could have answered some of Tevy's queries.

After a few moments, "Do you love me? "Tevy asks.

"I think I do,"I say.

"What about you?"I ask.

"I am not sure yet, but you fulfil my desire more than I supposed."

"What is stopping you from loving me," I ask.

"You are not very open as I am to you,I feel so."

"Is it?"I say.

"I feel you have something going within you detaining me to be fully accepted by you."

"I am divorced,"I say.

"What?"

"I was married once."

"Are you serious?"

"Yes,"

"You never told me you were married."

"I was waiting for the right time."

"Which is after having sex with me?"Tevy says furiously.

"No, I did not plan to have sex with you. It just happened,"I say.

"But you did plan to conceal the truth from me. It seems like all this is driven by intention."

"No, not at all," I say.

"Every encounter with you is making me feel more insecure about your love towards me. Even at this point in time, I am at crossroads in our relationship."

"I am in a complex relationship Tevy and do not intend to hide the truth from you. I loved my wife. She left me in the most absurd way one can imagine. I still have visions of her. I am worried about revealing anything about me or my past to you and thereby delving you into these dark feelings which I am gradually recovering from. I loved you and the few times we have been together. You look like Nila but you are nothing like her. Your personality and attitude are what I always wanted from Nila. She is quite complex and more than I can take. She is a sea of emotions. Her love is astounding and exhaustive. Her passions are boundless. She restricted my freedom with her excessively possessive nature. In the beginning, I adored her beauty and her incest. I enjoyed her company. Gradually I knew something about her that I was not aware of before. I could not take it anymore. She did not accept my refusal. She wanted me to surrender to her unconditionally. I still fear the moments we had in the past. She killed herself. I am horrified on that day. I am scared of her various facets of love. Until I have seen you, I never wished to be around any woman again, that was the impact of Nila on me. I cherished your presence. I was driven by your beauty and attitude. Though you look like Nila you revealed much more of yourself to me and impressed me. You filled the gap which Nila left. Gradually I found more of you which I am fond of. I stopped looking for the Nila I dreamed of in you. I embraced you as you are. Nila's love was conditional, but she needed me unconditionally. I could not surrender to her, felt choked.

Tevy drinks her coffee to the last drop in quick short sips. She walks into my room and changes back into her wet clothes. Without uttering a word, she exits from the main door closing with a dull thud. I feel relieved, not knowing why I felt so, maybe it was hard to explain what is going on inside me to her. I take a sip of my coffee. I walk towards the door and open it to see if she is still there or if anyone else is on the floor. There is an old man probably in his nineties sitting in a wheelchair and staring at me. His expression is neither curious nor disinterested it was somewhere in between. I leave the door open and walk into my unit.

Looking at my fish tank, I am very pleased. The two Oscars are graciously swimming along. I pick a can of live worms and feed them by hand. I clean the two empty plates later which were soiled with pasta remains. I stand in front of my bookshelf and pick up the book "Krishna, the man and his philosophy by Osho" and continue to read it from page 270 where I last left. I doze off into sleep after an hour of reading. I close my eyes and relax on the sofa. I sleep for the next couple of hours uninterrupted. I wake up and stare at my mobile.

"Are you free at 5 PM tomorrow?" asks Tevy in her text message to me

Am I free? Is there anything planned and decided in my life? I cannot be sure of it. However, my reply is going to have an impact in the future of our relationship. I wish to take no chances.

"I am fine to join tomorrow," I reply.

"Let's see."

The following day with no disruptions or visions engaging or polluting my head I proceed. We meet in the basement of our building.

"Let's go,"Tevy says.

"Are you okay with my scooter?"I ask.

"What's wrong with it ?"She asks.

"I mean I am not bringing my bike this time," I say.

"As long as it runs fine I do not mind, I am not a motorhead," She smiles.

"Alright then"

We head to a restaurant by the beach. As we walk in, we are impressed by the niche layout of a pub in the entrance hall but as we walk in the theme is conflicting. The designer got confused at a point if it is a fine dine-in or a pub. After our stride along the length of the restaurant, we notice the portico facing the beach of the restaurant is elegant and grand.

"Shall we have wine?"Tevy says.

We order a bottle of wine. After a few moments of silence, we decide to change the location to the garden of the restaurant facing the beach for a better mood. The menu has a myriad of drinks on the bar.

"Can we sit outside facing the beach?"I ask the bartender.

"Sure Sir. We can serve the drinks outside for you."He says.

"Thank you."

We take a seat closer to the beach. We sit on two bar stools instead of the laid-out chairs.

"Sorry Sir, this would not be covered as our premises. So we cannot serve here. If you wish to be seated here, you need to clear the bill Madam," The waiter says.

"Let me handle this," I say.

I walk inside to the billing counter and clear the bill.

"Hello Sir, we wish to see you again,"A man in a pin-striped suit says. He is in charge of the restaurant I suppose. Karim reads the name engraved on a tiny metal plate on his chest.

"Mr Karim, is there any possibility you can serve the drinks for us towards the end of your garden where the bar stools are placed?"I ask.

The waiter speaks to the manager softly in his ear probably repeating the context to him.

"Let me check Sir," Karim says.

In a few minutes, Karim says.

"We can let you sit there or on the beach and we will serve drinks and food for you, Sir, on a special request."

I walk outside to the garden.

"We can continue to order,"I say to Tevy as I sit beside her.

"Great!!"Tevy says.

"Can I ask you something?"

"Did you have any children with Nila?"

"No, we tried but it did not happen,"I say.

"Do you still see Nila in me?"

"Sometimes, I do but mostly these days I see you as you are."

"I still cannot commit to my relationship with you,"Tevy says.

"I can understand,"I say.

"I am unable to accept the fact that you did not tell me about Nila before,"Tevy says.

"It all happened too quickly, as a matter of fact, formally we never spoke about love or liking each other. We met at the beach and after a couple of drinks, it was too late to reveal anything."

"You could have stopped being intimate with me yesterday."

"I wish I could but,"I say not knowing how to finish that sentence.

Tevy Gulps Chardonnay instead of taking a sip as she usually did.

"I am going to Singapore,"Tevy says.

"You mean you are relocating?"

"No, it is just a client who needs me to explain our proposal, He does not have the time to come over to Malaysia. So my company promised to send an executive, which is me."Tevy says.

"So you got hired?"

"Yes I did, sorry I forgot to tell you that but for that, you are to be blamed."

"That's okay, Congrats,"I say.

"When are you leaving?"

"Two days from now I will decide on when to leave"

"Can I join you?"I ask.

"I wished to hear that from you. Thank you. Of course, you can,"Tevy says.

"My pleasure,"I say.

"I will decide shortly and tell you when we can start if you have any reservations do let me know I can consider the schedule."

"Okay"

"I am still sceptical about dating you,"Tevy says.

"Why?"

"I don't know,"

"I think I have married already in the past so."

"I wish it was that simple but something else is bothering me."

"Okay take your time."

"Thank you for trying to understand my situation," Tevy says.

"I am accommodating time for you to understand whatever the cause could be?"I ask.

"I was having all these visions Arka since we met. I am not sure if they are dreams or reality. If it was a dream, it should evaporate in the mundane activities of the day. Strangely all the dreams I have had since I met you persist in my memory. They do not vanish if it is a mere coincidence that you met me at the time when my mind got screwed up or if it were you the cause of it. Sorry to put it that way. I do not know what is the reason. I brushed off all this until recently and thought it could be due to stress at work. You did not stay away from me Arka. It was me who stayed away from you. These visions were so strong that I could not think of anything else but those faded glimpses along the day. Even more strangely I come across people I have in these visions," Tevy says

"If you are comfortable sharing," I say.

"I saw a river flowing towards me. The water was dark, and the flow is like a river. It had no colour but neither it is transparent. It was like the darkness of water seen in the night. I was not sleeping when I had this vision but rather sitting on my sofa during the day. It was the same sofa upon which we sat yesterday. I saw pitch-black darkness with my eyes wide open. That darkness would not exist even in the darkest of the night. As the river flowed towards me it was glistening with white reflections on the surface. I felt the river passing through my body. It filled my heart with sorrow for no specific reason I can figure out. It also made me feel pain as it rushed towards me, gradually it encircled me a few feet away. The dark water is now still, covering me hovering a hundred feet above me, it was like I was at the bottom of a well. I could see stairs along the length of the well, going down from where I am but nothing to go up. It had uprooted the deepest of melancholy from my heart as I placed my feet on the step and went down step by step. I traced the flesh of a human on my fingers. It was like dead meat. I could feel the face of the person by touching every detail of the skin on it. A long nose and a broad chin. In a minute, I could feel tears dropping on my fingers from those deep sunk eyes of the person. He was in deep sorrow and is whispering to me but I could not hear anything. After a while, I was lying flat on my sofa. I could see a little girl with red ribbons smiling at me. She pulled me out of the well and placed me on my sofa. She is laughing at me hysterically. I cannot detail to you what I felt then, maybe it is closer to shame. I felt violated by her as she tried to unbutton my dress. I was sobbing for the next few minutes. The little girl in red ribbons smiled at me standing a few feet away from me. She has red speckles on her face with a wheatish complexion and unkempt hair dangling from head to shoulders like spaghetti. She came forth and held my hand. I was drawn towards her. She invoked a feeling of compassion in me towards her. I hugged her with an urge unexplained. I was possessed I felt. In an instant, she was on my lap facing me tete-a-tete and whispering something into my ear. She is probably in her twenties now rapidly ageing in minutes. I did not like her touching me. I did not want that. She is kissing me passionately on my lips, and despite my fear towards her, I could not stop her as my body went numb with her touch, except for the brain. I did not want her. I have no desires towards women. I felt embarrassed. I tried to push her and escape but not futile. I fell unconscious on my sofa tired of signalling my mind to do something to resist but nothing happened in return as my body is out of my control. After a few minutes, I was lying again on my sofa. The teenager was nowhere to be seen. I could see myself dressed up all buttoned. There is no sign of pain in my body either. Is it a dream? I do not know I had the same dream thrice since I last met you at the beach. Sometimes these visions are so strong that I feel like I can get killed during the act due to the wild passion of the girl. I was hesitant to meet you for no particular reason. It was just that my gut felt not meeting you would help. When you stopped meeting me for a while these visions gradually reduced and I felt relieved."Tevy says.

"I am sorry to hear that, are your visions stopped now at once?"

"Yes, stopped for quite some time. I had one just today morning after we met yesterday."

"Maybe you should stop seeing me for a while,"I say.

"I wish I could do that, deep down in my heart, I need you,"Tevy says.

"I need you too," I say.

She moves her upper torso towards me and kisses my lips. I was in a bit awkward position to kiss sideways. We take a sip of wine. We ordered onion rings and sweet potato.

"I have many questions to ask you,"Tevy says.

"Go ahead."

"No, not today, I do not want to spoil our date further,"

Tevy says.

I smile at her.

"What brings that grin on your face"

"I never knew this was a date."

"Neither did I until we kissed,"

"I am going to ask one of my friends to lend their car to travel to Singapore," Tevy says.

"We can also hire one,"I say.

"Yeah either would be fine, Did you have any more headaches since yesterday"

"Not since I met you,"I say.

"I am afraid to delve into something I am not sure of. The only hope is you but sometimes I feel maybe I am too judgemental about our relationship. I have spoken about this already, and I know you would be embarrassed. I am trying to be open towards you. Though you give your complete attention to me, I still feel that you have something in you that despises me. If such a feeling exists, I want to know it now."Tevy says.

"There is no answer to that question. It is best to keep it unanswered. If I say that my feelings towards you are true at this point, it doesn't help you in any way. It will only make it difficult to part from me when you wish to. It would be better if you let time decide the fate of our relationship."I say.

"You speak wisdom all the time or only when you are completely drunk?"Tevy says laughing at me

"I am not fully drunk. It is best to keep the consequences of the wine on our thought process and thereby our relationship."

"So you say that my blabber when drunk can lead to a bleak possibility of crucifying our future?"

"Our blabber,"

We laugh at each other.

We walk along the shore. After a couple of drinks, the sunlight bends along the skyline reaching us and lighting up the harbour. A blend of crimson red and purple paints the sky during the golden hour. There are photographers lined up along the shore with grad filters mounted on their wide-angle lenses to capture the sunset. I wish I had my camera now. A splendid skyline with the shore blending with the colour. As I look into the rear of their camera LCDs I could see long exposures, colours altered by tweaking too much of white balance and those who just walk away with just a click in their phone camera. Tevy sways a bit as she walks, there is some amount of wine working on her. She also seems to be smiling more frequently than usual. Gradually, the evening light fades into the blue darkness, taking over the realm of the sky.

"Shall we go to a movie?"I ask.

"It would be a very bad idea. Whoever sits beside me has to bear the stench of my breath loaded with drinks."

"So we continue with the walk?"I ask.

"Yes please"

We walk for another 3 miles and find a nice spot to sit on the shore.

"What is your favourite colour?"Tevy asks.

"White,"I say.

"White?"

"Yes,"

"I thought you would say black."

"I find white more intriguing and complex to me than black," I say.

"What you say about white was my exact perception of black. So you like white since it is more complex ?"Tevy asks.

"Complexity is intriguing, and you never feel bored out of it,"I say.

"I hated black for being too complex and representing the dark side of anything. However, your description or opinion of white makes me reconsider."Tevy says.

"Maybe you can pick some other colour after all black and white are not the only ones," I say.

"Before that, I want to know why you dislike black."

"Black is everything. It is the colour of darkness. It has nothing onto itself. It is just void. It has no direction. It is what you perceive out of it. Like walking with your eyes closed and imagining whatever lays ahead of you."I say.

"So your fears are what is putting that colour away,"Tevy asks.

"I am not afraid of the dark Tevy. The greatest of fears are no longer in the darkness. They monger in the light. Everyone fears the dark and is repulsive to it. Trust me it is not as scary as the day."I say.

"DO you still call this a date?"Tevy asks.

"You were the one asking the questions,"I say.

"What is your favourite food?"She asks.

"There you go, another question,"I say.

"Answer it."

"I like lamb with mandi rice."

"Anything lighter than that?"

"Spaghetti"

"Let us go and have some. I am hungry now,"Tevy says laughing at me

We trace back our path until we reach the restaurant. I order spaghetti for both of us, and Tevy adds a mashed potato side to it.

"It was fun,"Tevy says.

"The talk ?"I ask.

"The walk, I never walked so long after finishing a bottle of wine," Tevy says.

We smile at each other.

"You have your family here?"Tevy asks.

"I am all alone by myself, I do have a few relatives in India. They take care of my property and the rentals I get from it. The major portion of my earning comes from there. My parents died when I was young. My mother had cancer and when she died my father could not take it anymore, he succumbed to excessive alcohol intake."

"I wish I should not have asked you that question, Sorry."

"That's perfectly fine. It happened too fast when I was young. I hardly remember those days now. My grandmother who took care of me died a few weeks after my wedding. That was the moment I could not control my emotions. She died naturally. We were very poor when young. My father made some good investments and took calculated risks to earn money, when everything was going fine, my mother was diagnosed with cancer. The whole world seemed to have fallen apart. I do remember that day when my dad stopped smiling. He stood strong for her until the last moment. He spent every penny to save her. My dad loved my mom against the will of his parents. After their refusal of his marriage, he moved out. He never sought help from his parents, but I remember he did once when my mother was sick. They heard all he said and his situation and responded by saying that he could have heeded their advice based on astrology regarding his marriage, and their compatibility and avoided this situation by not marrying my mother. My father could not take their comments lightly he walked away never to return to them again. Later he files a case in court on his rightful property to be inherited from his grandfather. By the time he received the verdict or owned the property, I had lost both my parents. I also lost my paternal grandparents who could not take the early death of their son easily. The court ruled the case was closed and transferred the assets to me as the legal heir. My maternal grandmother was the only person who took care of me all the while."I say.

"I am very sorry," Tevy says sinking into deep thought.

"How about your family?"I ask

"Your food is here Sir"Interrupts the waiter.

"This is fish and chips, did we order this?" I ask Tevy.

"The table number matches Sir. It Could be that you pressed in the iPad wrongly, Can I have a look?"

"We did not use the iPad to place the order,"I say.

"Apologies Sir" Let me check right away and get back to you

The table beside us is seated by an aged American couple. They possibly overheard the conversation.

"That fish and chips belong here," says the American man.

"This spaghetti should have been there," His wife adds to his statement.

"Sorry for the confusion, I just joined today," says the waiter as he swaps the dishes across the tables.

We smile at the couple as the waiter leaves. Aware of the feeling that the couple can hear our conversation we finish our food in silence.

We travel back on my Burgman scooter, at a speed of 80 miles per hour while driving I see Nila walking in the opposite direction of the road. Startled I hit the brakes slamming Tevy on my back.

"I am sorry," I say.

"I was sleeping, thanks for alerting me to stay awake," Tevy says.

A line of cars already started honking behind me. I watch Nila walking past us. Nila confronts me only when she is concerned about something. It must be Tevy who could be bothering her. I fear her existence and appearance, despite her death but I am not going to give up my freedom either. I like Tevy she is my future and my life. I start the bike and head forward. We reach home and I park the bike at the same spot where I picked it up in the morning. We say bye to each other on my floor at the escalator. I head to my flat hoping that I do not see Nila hanging like before. Fortunately, everything is normal. I sit in my chair near the window. I grab my mobile from my pocket and install some apps. I am still not inclined towards the very popular social media apps. I go for a bath, humidity and wine created some discomfort in me. Post that, with nothing to do I send a Good Night text message to Tevy and go to bed.

Around 3 AM, I feel someone trying to undress me. My shirt buttons are pulled off, not by me. Someone is licking the tip of my penis and I am all hard. Lying flat on my bed I look at the hair falling like a fountain and resting on my groin. She is moving her head like a pendulum while I am relishing in paradise. What seemed happening in a dream before in a state of ecstasy, is now happening in real. I jump from my bed instantly throwing the woman off the bed. I turn on the lights to see Nila.

"Stop this I do not like it,"I say.

"Liars, both of you,"Nila says.

"Just go,"I say.

"You want to have sex with that new smug face girlfriend of yours, don't you? Trust me she is not as good as she seems to be," Nila says.

"Stop it. I do not want to hear any more of your nonsense,"I say.

"You never had an ear for me,"Nila says.

"Stop bothering her, you have no right to abuse her,"I say.

"Neither do you," Nila says.

"I like her also she does like me," I say.

"If that is true, I have every right to her, "Nila says.

"I have encouraged you all those years and paying the price for it, Leave me, I need my life."

"You always got whatever you wanted, it was me who sacrificed for your selfishness."

"You cheated upon me,"I say.

"I never slept with any other man. I never stole your money nor did I swindle,"Nila says

"You betrayed me. You never loved me, our marriage was for society,"I say,

"How many times should I repeat that I loved you with all my heart?" Nila says.

"So did you to that girlfriend of yours,"I say.

"You still mind that?"Nila says.

"No matter how much you try to hack my mind, I can never forget the fact that you are bisexual and you are a woman predator," I say.

"You blew the issue out of proportion. You wanted to get rid of me so you did,"Nila says.

"You think you shared your love? No, you betrayed,"I say.

"Our relationship never had a future. You never really liked me, "Nila says.

"That is not true, I loved you over the top of this world. You slept with random women. I was shocked when I saw you and the helper woman in the room. Do you think all that is nothing? No, it is not. It is infidelity. I can never be the same after that. Yet I never have divorced you. I took care of you as a husband."

"I never loved any of them more than you, you are the only man and real partner in my life, "Nila says.

"Yes I do agree you have never been with any other man, but there is a correction it does not mean you have love towards me, it is lust."

"I never loved those women Arka. I had a lust for other women I agree but I always loved you."

"What do you want me to do now?"I say,

"I know you no longer love me or care for me."

"I did love you."

"So you stopped now for that pretty face you are after? Do not do this for your needs. I will take care of you. Do not feel that I cannot satisfy your sexual desires. I can control your mind and give you the same pleasure or maybe multifold better feeling than that woman of yours who barely has anything to engage you for a while."

"Stop it, Nila, not everyone, is a predator like you. Nor am I after her for her body. I am feeling pure love and real happiness with her which you can never do in my mind with your tricks. I longed for such feelings from you but in vain. You were neither true to yourself nor me. All you did was manipulate me to accept your ways after marriage."

"I am manipulative? So be it,"Nila says.

"What now? What else can you do?"

"Let me show you the manipulations you talk about to your sick girlfriend," Nila says.

"Threatening me is not going to make anything better, it will only make me despise you even more"

"How about this? Your girlfriend who already seems to keep away from you, sensing trouble, is now going to get a good dose of my treatment. Let us see how long she can sustain."

"Stop it, do not harm her, she is innocent, this is what I am talking about, your evil ways came out and real colours shown in no time."

"You call me evil? If I wish I can do anything to your doll and keep her away from you forever. I know you like her. I do not want to spoil your sport. I checked up on her. Trust me, she is not going to last for long. She is the type who runs away from trouble. You cannot count on her. I am here for you even after death. Do you know the worth of it? You must be proud to have me watching your back.

"You have the thoughts to eliminate her. I know you would not stop here," I say.

"If you know and genuinely care for her, you won't love her or get into this mess but you will do coz you are the most self-centred person who is equally pretentious trying to be on good terms with everyone. You have a poker face, so you live, I do not, so I succumbed. We both are the same Arka, trust me you are no better than me," Nila says.

"I do not seek any attention. If that is the case, leave me. Did I ask you to love me or protect me? If you despise me so be it, stay away. Be what you are and go after what you want. Rest in peace, Nila."

"I never said I despised you. I meant you are like me. Your gamble with words is not going to drive me anywhere. I will stay with you forever. Anyone who stops will have to face the wrath of my curse. Let me finish what I have started." Nila says.

"What?"

"Relax darling. I mean let me finish off my work down your pants and then you can sleep like a baby."

"Go away,"I say.

I turn off all the lights, walk towards the refrigerator and drink some chilled water. I notice that my erection is gone.

I jump into my bed again and roll the sheets over me trying to get some sleep.

I hear a chime on my mobile at 5 AM but I continue to sleep. I get some nightmares about Nila trying to harass Tevy. I am aware at the back of my mind somehow this is a dream and I stop worrying. With my body turning numb and no sensation whatsoever, I sleep like a baby.

CHAPTER SIX

1970 Khmer Republic (Cambodia)

Narrator: Heng Chann

Sorya is unconscious and lying in my cart. Kala is approaching. I decided to inform her about her husband's condition since she would be more worried later when she discovers him missing.

"Kala" I scream at her standing like a dwarf from my elevated view in the cart.

"Yes brother," Kala says.

"Your husband is unconscious, we need to take him to the hospital," I say.

"What?"

"Yes, Sorya is sick we need to take him to the hospital."

"Okay I will tend to him at home."

"No, he is in the cart right now. We have no time, please get in,"I say.

"Okay," Kala says as she moves to the rear to find Sorya and starts to weep

"He is unconscious, what happened to him, brother tell me the truth what happened?"Kala says sobbing profusely,

"Please control Kala, nothing has happened, he is just unconscious and is still fine," I say.

While she continues with her grieving, I focus on speeding towards the hospital. I have never been to the city and do not know where the hospital is. Anyway, in such a place, I think asking someone can help. At once I felt to take him to Yiey, but I was worried if that old woman can be of any help in this critical situation.

I am now riding the cart like a warrior heading for a battle upon the attack signal. As we arrive at the counter made of mud walls and a wooden roof beside the Mekong rover I stop the cart.

"How much,"I ask the person at the counter.

"Three of you,"He asks,

"Yes"

"What happened to him"

"He is unconscious."

"You are not disposing of him in the river are you?" He laughs at me.

"I will punch your face so that you can never show those ugly teeth again to anyone,"I say furiously.

Without uttering a word, he takes the money and directs his hand to another person near the boat signalling him a go-ahead for three.

We cautiously step onto the boat managing to lift Sorya by the arms, while the person on the boat holds his legs towards the bent knees. Kala is still in a state of shock, her stare is elsewhere, and she might be going through a sea of emotions. As we wade into the water on the boat, we notice Champa coming in the opposite direction. She is holding two bulging big bags while another two more are on her back.

"Kala" Champa screams at her.

As Kala looks at Champa her sobbing intensifies multifold and begins to weep louder, maybe she found someone to share her feelings with. Champa signals the rower, and he moves the tip of the boat parallel to our boat.

"Take this stuff to the shore and leave it at the counter."Champa shouts at the rower.

"Keep this stuff until I come."Champa shouts to the counter.

She raises her leg and with precision jumps into the middle of our boat, causing our boat to sway a bit randomly.

"What happened," Champa asks.

"He is lying like this,"Kala says with tears in her eyes.

Kala looks at me for an answer with a stare.

"He had a stroke or seizure I am not very sure when I saw him he was lying on the ground in his house unconscious, he can be normal in some time," I say.

"How do you know brother?" Kala asks,

"It did happen to him in the past,"I say.

"Which means he had this problem all the while but did not tell me,"Kala asks.

"Yes he did but he got it recently, I believe we do not waste time further and take him to the hospital," I say this signalling the rower to move ahead.

"How about you?"I ask Champa.

"I am coming with you,"She says.

"Alright," I say feeling a sense of relief since I have never been to the city earlier.

As the boat moves, I feel a tinge of surprise within me as I see the grass along with the river swaying and the cool breeze coming from the other direction runs through my hair. I have never been out of the village until now. This is a new experience and it is refreshing though the reason I am going is constricting me to express my feelings. Kala seems still worried but much better after Champa joined us. Champa is looking at me while I look elsewhere and I could figure it out. I think she loves me. She is consoling Kala as and when possible. When Kala was not gazing at her, she placed her finger under the nose of Sorya to check his breath. The dark clouds are foraging the sky and the wild creepers running along the length of the river. The man rowing the boat has a face in his eighties while his body is having the fitness of a young man.

"Have you been to the city before?"Champa asks.

"Never been there," I say.

"Good that we met before you leave"

"Is the city so confusing?"

"You can navigate and get along but since this is your first visit, substantial time would be lost in figuring routes around."

"We are fortunate to have you with us."

Kala folds her arms in a gesture referred to as Sampea indicating her thankfulness to Champa. However, due to her Indian origin, her gesture is more like a Namaste of Hindu origin. The boat glides along the river. The water is muddy at the shallow spots and clear when deep.

"Get down," says the boat punter

"Can you help me with the foot?"I say.

"Sure, give me a minute,"The punter says.

We hold him by the knees and shoulder and place him on the bank of the river. As we do so, I accidentally stumble upon a stone and drop Sorya closer to the ground scraping it slightly and lifting him back again.

Sorya now moves his shoulder while his eyes remain closed. Like a baby who woke up from a dream, Sorya opens his eyes staring directly at me.

Kala chants some prayers thanking God.

"Where are we?"Sorya asks.

"We are about to go to the city," I say.

"City? Why?"

"Will tell you later,"I say,

"We have to see the doctor,"Kala says.

"Yes we should,"I repeat.

"Doctor?"Sorya asks.

"Yes, you think you are superhuman?"Kala asks.

"I never said that I was a normal human and humans suffer inevitably at some point so we need not take this more seriously, go back home,"Sorya says.

"You better stay silent and follow us."Kala raises her voice. Her voice is deep with sorrow coming out of a choked throat.

I look at the punter who is completely puzzled by our conversations. I grasp his look and step ahead to pay Kak to him since he is noticeably awaiting his payment.

"That's okay," Champa says to me.

"I do not get it,"I say.

"We have pre-paid trips. This can get covered,"Champa says.

"Let it be,"I say as I pay him.

"How do we go from here?" I ask.

"Go where,"Sorya asks.

I shrug at him.

"Hospital," says Kala in a firm voice.

We follow her on the road with crushed and softened stones, unlike the mud road in our village. The city was fascinating the children are walking on the roads as adults do. They are not afraid of walking alone. In our village, small children rely on their parents to go anywhere only for playing in the neighbourhood or at the river, they go alone. Two boys were carrying coloured toys. In the village, toys are mostly made of clay and not coloured.

"What is that made of?"I ask.

"It is made of plastic," Champa says.

"How much it costs?"I ask.

"It is quite costly usually found with the kids of parents from an elite background," Champa says.

"I see."

"I am trying to get some of those toys to sell in our village, yet to figure out if there is a demand for it," Champa says.

Kala upon hearing us observes the toy now.

"Is there anything bothering you?"I ask Kala.

"Yes, Kids I forgot about them. They would be crying and waiting for me" Kala says.

"We need to go back,"Sorya says.

"No let us go to the doctor and then we can go back, they play until night and would hardly need us. I told our neighbour Bopha to look after them. They will be safe at their place. If we are not home, she will keep the kids with her."

Followed by silence, all of us head towards the hospital.

The hospital is stretching four blocks long. It is the largest building I saw until now. I knew it was the hospital as I saw people walking in the garden accompanied by nurses. The atmosphere is very calm. Most of the patients outside the hospital are old. There are large portraits of a man in a gold and black suit hung on the walls.

"The king,"Champa says.

"Oh, so he is the King everyone talks about,"I stare at the portrait and speak in a spell.

"This is the first time I am seeing him,"I say.

"The people here know him very well."

"Who is the sick one?" says the Nurse with her hair neatly shoved into a single plait hanging on her back like a pony.

Sorya moves forward to her.

"Please follow me," She says.

"I am having a problem with..."Sorya says.

"Please wait here, we will call you,"Nurse says interrupting Sorya.

We walk closer towards Sorya and stand beside him as he sits on the wooden bench.

"Is this needed ?"Sorya asks.

"Yes it is,"Kala said.

After waiting for an hour, we get to the point of not knowing what we are here for nor thinking of going back before the purpose we were here. We have no intention of going back since there is a high chance that Sorya can have the stroke again.

Patients kcep flooding the hospital, and most of them are coughing. We doubt if any doctor is tending to the patients or if the patients are leaving after long hours of waiting. None of the patients leaving the consultation room is smiling. The ones who entered with a smile also came out with various shades of sadness embossed on their face. The hospital windows are thick with layers of dust. Birds nested in almost all the window shelters.

"Please come in," says the attendant to Sorya

As we move ahead, she interrupts again.

"Only the patient," She says.

"Sorry, I have to go along with him, "Kala says.

"Not allowed," the nurse says.

"I did not ask for your permission, I told you, "Kala says.

"You have to follow the rules here."

"Let the doctor tell me to go out,"Kala says and walks along

with Sorya unheeding her instruction.
The attendant walks over to stop Kala but she quits as Kala enters the doctor's chamber along with Sorya.

After twenty long minutes, Sorya and Kala came out. While Kala is sad and bearing an expression similar to those who came earlier, Sorya is smiling.

"What happened, "I ask.
"The doctor said I needed to be admitted here."
"Why?"
"He needs to look into the details of my case and take some reports, he thinks I need to be referred to a specialist based on his analysis."
"If she cannot diagnose you why should you get admitted here,"I ask.
"He will arrange for qualified doctors to come from the West."
"Let us go home, I cannot afford it anyways,"Sorya says.
"Will you please stop making statements?"Kala says.
"I know someone in the city," Champa says.
"Doctor?"I ask.
"No, but they can help us find the right one," Champa says.
"Are you sure?"I ask.
"Yes"
"I will do something if it is about affording the costs," Kala says.
"Sorry Kala, I did not mean that, in the city, many try to cheat us when they figure out where we came from. We should try to approach people who stay here and get their help so that we do not end up swindled,"Champa says.
"Okay Champa, I trust your advice," Kala says.
We walk two kilometres from there and then reach an old building with a gate covered in freshly coated paint. The walls are clad in pure white. I make the finest contact

with my finger on the gate avoiding too much contact and pushing it hard. The lawn is lush with green moist moss and plants. The place is wet and damp. We walk towards the door of the house. I get a weird feeling of isolation surrounding the atmosphere of the house. It is nothing like the neighbourhood. The rooms inside the building are lit with warm lights deflecting through the glass panes embedded in the doors facing us.

"Looks like there is no one inside," I say.

"Wait here," Champa says as she walks around the house.

We stand on the porch while Champa walks around to find someone. After a few minutes, a door opens in front of us.

"Who are you?" a woman probably in her fifties with a white wrinkled face, random red flakes on her cheeks and grey hair opens the door and asks us.

Kala walks over to call Champa while I respond to her.

"We are from a nearby village. Champa got us here," I say.

"Champa? Who is she?"asks the old woman staring at the fingers on her feet seems like she is counting them or recollecting the name Champa.

Champa walks over to us.

"Oh dear girl, how are you? Did you stop eating? You look so weak,"says her to Champa, she probably recognized her.

"Hello Mother, how are you, where is Father? I am fine eating more than usual,"Champa says.

"Come inside everyone"

We finally feel relieved that someone accepted us in a strange city. As we walk inside huge curtains, beautifully decorated walls and exquisite furniture, and painted glass windows, with attendants guarding the house at all corners reveal to us. It was the complete opposite of what we perceived from the outside. It was ironic that it took so long for them to open the door with so many inside.

"Had your food, everyone?" She asks.

"We did,"I say.

"We have left kids at home so have to leave a bit early," Kala says.

"Yes Mother, we need to go early today" Champa affirms

"Alright," She says as she signals one of the attendants towards a room.

In a few minutes, women attendants accompanied by a butler walk towards us with a large-sized silver plate decorated with bread and pastries.

"Please have them. My uncle got these from France," She says.

"Thank you," we respond in synchrony and fetch one each from the plate.

"My name is Chenda by the way," says the lady to the rest of us.

"Who are they?"I whisper at Champa, seeing Chenda leave the room.

"They are relatives of the royal family," Champa says.

"What?"

"Yes you heard it right,"Champa says.

"How do you know them?"I ask in a soft tone.

"They found me selling stuff in the city in the past and since have been nice to me, they are intrigued by my boldness as a woman to leave the village and work here They invited me to visit their home sometimes as a gesture of their friendly relationship."

Chenda returns with more servants getting more snacks.

"Please feel at home and have them,"Chenda says.

"Thank you, Madam," Kala says.

"Why are all of you standing, please sit down, "Chenda says.

I sit on the sofa. The arms of it are of dark wood neatly polished and shining like the night sky. I am pleasantly surprised by the grandeur of the house and the intricate details of everything inside. The cushion on the chair is like it was embossed into the wood, I have never seen such finishing or workmanship till now.

"What about Father where is he?"

"I do not know Champa. He has not come home for more than twenty days. I am worried about him. We had also set up a search party to find him. Something is going on in the city. The town council is not trustworthy. They always seem to be plotting on the royal family. I see dark clouds looming upon us time and again. By the way, why are you in the city?"Chenda asks.

"These are my friends, Madam, they live in the village. Sorya is Kala's husband, and he is having a medical condition and needs help. I guided them to the hospital and was asked to admit Sorya. They spoke a great deal about his condition and we are not sure how much it would cost. Also, Kala has her kids at home, and we cannot admit him immediately," Champa says.

"You have the best doctor at home already and you believe these folk in the city?" Chenda chuckles at us

"Yiey?"I ask.

"Of course, Yes!"Chenda says.

"She has saved many from their deathbeds. I do not trust the practitioners in the city. They go by a checklist to determine if you are sick or not. If you do not fit into any of their criteria, they are baffled and confuse your body and mind with medicines. However, I will recommend you to the doctor as you insist. He has a clinic at his home. He also works at the hospital. He will not admit you unless there is a real need, I will send an attendant with you to assist. Post his consultation if he recommends you to get admitted then you probably should. Consult him first. The name of the doctor is Sokema, and he lives two lanes away from here. An attendant will update me on the status, so you can go back to the village today. I will make the needed arrangements as needed," Chenda says.

"Thank you very much, Madam," Kala says folding her hands.

Chenda smiles at her.

"Champa please wait, let me get something for all of you," Chenda says.

In a few minutes, a leather bag is passed on to Champa brimming with fruits and clothes.

"Thank You," Champa says.

"That's Okay, come home often,"Chenda says.

A man in a white bush shirt and gold stripes running along the shoulder and a metal clasp on his chest joins us as we step outside.

"Please follow me,"He says.

We follow him without questioning further. The sky is drizzling as we walk along. The velocity of the raindrops is consistent yet the size is increasing gradually. They are getting bulbous and pinching hard onto the skin. The attendant walks unperturbed by the rain. His pace is swift, and we were unable to catch up with him. Kala is concerned about that.

"Can we walk faster?" I say.

Like a guard dog waiting for a command, the man runs like a cheetah. He is waiting for the order. We burst into laughter seeing him run. We hop over the patches of wet mud in between troughs filled with rainwater. Kala and

Sorya try to catch up with the man sparing a few steps and splashing mud into the feeble air in the rain. I am slowing down to avoid slipping into the muddle. Champa is not athletic and is not a very good runner. Though she seems to be enjoying the chase. I raised the speed to my stride to catch up with Kala so that we are not lost. To avoid a muddle I stretch my leg more than I probably should, the foot of my right foot could not grasp the ground to anchor my next step. My foot slips, and I do a split falling into the mud. I am shocked at that moment. Champa was walking behind me. She runs to grab my shoulder and laughs at me.

"You wanted to run fast? Didn't you?"Champa says with a giggle."

"I wanted to catch up with Kala," I say.

"I knew you would fall. I was moving slowly to avoid this,"Champa says.

"Is there anything you don't know?"I say embarrassed that she laughed at me.

"I never knew your fall would be so funny,"Champa says as I am listening to her feeling funny and stupid.

"Very funny," I say.

"The last time I fell was it not this funny"Champa says.

"What? You also fell?"I burst into laughter, as she smiles along with me.

"We lost track of them"

"Do not worry I am aware of the location of the clinic," Champa says,

"Then why did you ask for the servant?"

"A representative from the royal family expedites our work," Champa says.

"You are wise," I say.

"Do not keep staring at your pants, there is a well nearby and you can wash. Being wet should not be an issue since it is raining and people do not stare at you at the clinic" Champa says.

"Alright, thanks," I say.

We walk slowly now.

"Did you think of me?" Champa asks.

"Think? About you?"I ask.

"Yes about us"

"I like you,"I say.

"Can you marry me?" she asks.

"I cannot be fooled like this. I have feelings,"I say.

"Fool you? You remember what has happened between us, don't you? Why will I fool you? You don't like me now?"

"You have everything, Champa, you have beauty and brain. I do not have anything. I was born poor and never left the village until today. Your house is ten times bigger than my hut.You can get a suitable and rich man who takes good care of you," I say.

"Do you love me or not?"Champa asks

"I can't love you. I have lost everyone till now. I loved my baby sister. She is nowhere closer to me. I lived a life with my friend beside and now Sorya is ill he is the only one I had all day to share my thoughts and routine. I love you more than ever Champa but I fear that happiness is never my destiny, I do not want to pull you into my ill fate. I deceived you by having a physical relationship. You can shame me in public for whatever I did but do not crucify your happy life being with me."I say.

"Even if whatever you said is what you meant, I have no life without you Chann. I liked you for what you are. There is sincerity in you, unblemished by the colours painted upon by society. You are untouched by the cold feelings of the wicked crowd. I cannot stand to live with a person who knows how to put up an act. I have observed you for a long time I have also hurt you with my words. I thought you like most of the men but you are different, I felt I can live with you forever. If you do not accept me, I will remain single forever," Champa says.

"What's up with you? Are you guys coming?"Sorya shouts at us from a distance.

Sorya, who initially opposed the idea of consulting the doctor, seems to have forgotten about it and gave in completely to the decision of Kala.

"We are coming,"I respond.

"What happened to you?" Sorya asks staring at my pants.

It seems to me that this misunderstanding between Sorya and me is intentionally ignored by him. Even I pretend to accept his conversation as if there was nothing between us.

"I just fell into the mud," I say.

"Are you okay or hurt anywhere?"

"I think I am finc."

"The well?"I ask Champa.

"Please walk, it is nearby," Champa says.

We continue to make short jumps avoiding ditches of mud and water. I could see the clinic in front of me but yet there is no sign of the well.

"GO ahead for a few more feet from here," Champa says.

I stare at her with a blank gaze.

"Never mind I will come over to help you," Champa says.

"Can you wait in the lobby?" Champa says to Sorya.

"Alright but please make it fast, the royal guard is in a rush to talk to the doctor and go home"

"Will be back in no time"

We keep walking further trying to recollect the topic where we were interrupted.

"I need some time,"I say,

"For what?"Champa asks.

"To decide,"I say.

We walk a few feet ahead and as we reach the well. I stand at the edge of it dropping the empty bucket inside. I angle the bucket so that it can take a slight dip thereby making it sink further by the weight of water gained and make it full. I retrieve the bucket.

"Give me the bucket"Champa splashes the water on my pants and onto the back of my shirt targeting the spots stuck with mud. As the stains are hard, she places her hand on me and rubs.

I take off my shirt and with minor traces of the brown remains, still there, I try to wash and wear it again.

"Much better than before," I say.

"As you say,"Champa says.

We walk back to the hospital. As we walk inside, Champa does a quick check on the visitors outside to find Kala.

"This way" The Royal Guard comes out of nowhere and leads us.

He walks straight to the doctor's chamber though many are outside waiting. As he opens the door, we see Kala and Sorya inside.

"Please wait outside,"Doctor says.

"That should be okay there are family," the guard says to the doctor.

"We will wait outside," I say signalling Champa to come with me.

"No please stay,"Doctor says to us.

Though I could see Sorya was a bit uncomfortable about it.

"I prefer we stay outside," I say.

"Okay," the doctor says.

After waiting outside for several minutes, the guard seems to be disappointed by my decision. He did not like standing amidst patients.

"How long would they take?"Champa asks,

"Maybe it is the doctor's decision,"I say.

Finally, after thirty minutes of general consultation, they come outside.

"What happened?"Champa asks Kala.

Kala ignores her questions, walks a few feet towards the entrance where there are fewer people and then replies to her.

"We need not to admit to the hospital today," Kala says.

"Thank God," Champa says.

"However the situation is not so the good doctor says, Sorya has a disease which affects the brain and could lead to loss of memory gradually,"Kala says bursting into tears.

Champa embraces her with a tight hug. The guard is startled by the situation and is confused about how to react.

I and Sorya walk along the hallway to the entrance on the grass.

"I am sorry Sorya, "I say.

"Sorry for what? I am not going to die soon," Sorya says.

"No, I was very mean to you. Whatever you spoke was the truth about my parents and my childhood, your perspective could be right, I should have had the right state of mind to understand what you were saying,"I say.

"Don't worry Chann. It is now clinically proved that I am not in the right state of mind, so maybe your reaction is justified,"Sorya says.

"What did the doctor say?"I ask.

"He did not conclude anything. Could be there is no cure for the disease. He did not rush me to get treatment immediately. He encouraged me to live happily and to live in the present."

"How could he not give treatment to you, in such a critical condition?" I ask.

"Maybe he is right Chann, I needed him more than the so-called doctors who use all their studies to treat me without considering my feelings. I felt the doctor knew I am more interested in living life fully for whatever time I still have."Sorya says

We remain silent for the next twenty minutes inspecting the grass without a microscope.

Kala and Champa walked out. I can make out that Kala had a very emotional moment. Her face is bloated eyes red, her hair unkempt and her cheeks pale.

The royal guard walks towards the payment counter and without much discussion gives a broad smile. I never knew he could smile, his facial structure seemed to lock those flexors which enabled it. He did put in some effort.

"We have cleared the payment process can go," the royal guard says.

"Thank You,"I say.

"I will accompany you till the boat terminal,"He says.

We silently follow the royal guard who is less frustrated and more hospitable in his approach this time. Suffering can derive pity from anyone. We wait for some time at the terminal where we are away from the queue.

The royal guard talks to the person at the counter. He smiles again as he did at the hospital and has a small chat with the person at the desk.

The boats from the villages reach the terminal. Everyone rushes forward picking up their stuff in jute bags.

"You there, come over" the person at the counter waves his hand at us directing us to skip the queue and onboard.

There is no protest challenging us to skip the queue. We onboard the first boat and the rest are allowed to onboard onto other boats. The river is brownish with mud on the surface probably agitated due to the rain and wind.

"Heading to?"

"Roka," Champa says.

The boat glides smoothly with one single stroke of the oar running deep into the water.

Somehow I feel better going back to the village, Maybe this could be the feeling of anyone going home after a while for the first time.

We get down at the terminal and head to the cart on which I drove Sorya and Kala. I help Champa fetch her stuff from the counter and load it into the cart. I did not ask her if she would come with us, it was implicit I suppose.

With Kala, Sorya and Champa on the cart, I am confused about where to head first.

"The kids would be alone and waiting,"Kala says.

It was dusk and turning out to be darker every minute.

"Champa is it okay if it gets a little late? I ask.

"I can manage at home," Champa says.

"Alright then" I trigger the oxen to head in the direction leading to Kala's house. It would have been the shorter distance to drop Champa first. I did not debate as Champa would be with me for a little longer which I cherish."

We reach the house of Kala after passing mine.

"Get down," I say to Champa as she is sitting at the end of the cart.

"Where are the kids?"Sorya asks for the first time raising concern about them.

"You left home later than me," says Kala sarcastically.

"Let me fetch the kids. I know where they are,"Sorya says.

"Yes please, let me cook food for all of you by then, "Kala says.

"No, it is already late, Yiey would worry about me, it is time for me to start,"Champa says.

"Please have dinner and go," Kala says.

"I will come home for dinner or lunch some other day," Champa says.

Champa stares at me signalling offline if I could drop her.

"I will drop Champa and come back," I say.

"Let her have some snacks and juice at least, "Kala says.

Kala brings some fish and tapioca crackers for us to eat. Champa has a few of them hastily.

"How is Yiey's health ?"Kala asks.

"She is fine, but age is making her mind go crazy sometimes," Champa says.

This was the first time I heard Champa complaining about Yiey in front of me. I was never having such a privilege. Champa is more patient with me and her change of perception towards me is evident.

"Much better than other old women of her age," Kala says.

"My expression is understated, she is at par with them," Champa says.

Kala smiles at her.

"I shall leave then," Champa says.

"Let me drop you, not sure if Sorya will come anytime soon,"I say.

"You can take the cart and drop her brother. He will take time and probably have his dinner at the neighbour's house, they will not let him leave without supper,"Kala says.

"Alright then, "I say.

We walk out of the house towards the entrance.

I mount at the rider's seat while Champa sits towards the end of the cart.

"You know the way?"Champa asks.

"Sorry, I could not hear you,"I say.

Champa moves nearer to me by crawling up in the cart.

"You know the route?"

"Yes, I remember vaguely."

"What occurred to Sorya is quite bad," Champa says.

"Yes that was the last thing on my mind that he would have at his age," I say.

"So what do you plan to do about it?"Champa asks.

The dangling bells of the belt strapped to the neck of the ox are usually harmonious but now it seems to be a nuisance as it interrupts the voice of Champa talking to me.

"I am not very sure," I say.

"You will need to take him to the hospital again," Champa says.

"Why?"I ask.

"That doctor does not give complete information to the direct dependents to avoid panic," Champa says.

"I will talk to Sorya again, and we will go together,"I say.

"I will join you if possible."

"I wish you do,"I say.

"I would be coming for Sorya and not for someone who does not have the intention of living with me, whatever could be the reason,"Champa says.

I remain silent pretending that I did not hear her.

"Stop here," Champa says as we near her house.

There is a dim light on the front wall of their house. Yiey seems to be lurking around there. Champa jumps to the ground from the cart and walks hastily towards the entrance. As she nears her house, the light brightens up, it is an oil lamp held in the hands of Yiey. I could now see at least a dozen men and women beside Yiey. All of them are staring at me. They are intrigued by my presence now.

"Hey come over here," shouts someone from the crowd at me.

Champa talks to him which I could only see. Yeiy is furious at Champa, which again I can only see from a distance.

"Let him go," says Yiey to the person in the crowd.

I get down from the cart trying to explain them. By the moment I approach, some of them dispersed from the place and the rest walked inside the house. I feel it is not necessary to confront them anymore. I get onto my cart again and head back.

I am in my bed on the floor, sometimes the life we sought after becoming a reality. But then we fear a reality. I was thinking to marry Champa till the very moment she asked me to. Only when she did, I realized my friend's misfortune knocking often at my door. I try not to think of her, but she pops into my mind. I do not want her to suffer with me. She can get someone much better than me. I should have backed off on that night. It would be cruel to cheat upon her now as the way everyone sees it. If I count each thought in my mind and associate it with a star in the sky it would reach a million. Hope the day which clears the stars in the sky also gives clarity to my thoughts. I sleep with my eyes open at the entrance of my hut smiling at the wide-open sky.

"Haven't slept yet ?" looming out of the darkness Sorya walks over.

"No," I say sitting on my bed and looking at him.

"Come over, sit,"I say,

"I have got something special for us."

"What is that?"

"Rice wine,"He says as he picks a glass bottle with transparent liquid mounted in his trouser.

"Any occasion,"I ask.

"Yes today is the fourth day of the third week of this month,"He says and laughs at me.

"How is that special?"I ask.

"Stop pestering me with your questions, I made it up,"Sorya says.

"Wait," I say and walk inside to get two glasses and a cask of water.

"That is better,"Sorya says.

"Chann, did you like her?"Sorya asks

"I do"

"Did you propose to her?"

"No, I think it is not a wise idea."

"I can talk to her. We can get the help of Kala to also convince. I know you like her I can see it in your eyes. She needs time probably."

"You saw that in her eyes?"I ask.

"Yes"

"If so your perception of eyes is inaccurate," I say.

"Let me have a drink to comprehend your speech,"Sorya says.

"You say that she does not need time. She decided not to marry you"

"Yes and No,"I say.

"Yes for what"

"Yes for she does not need time and No for she decided not to marry me,"I say.

"What? Is it not what you wanted? You are the one supposed to offer a drink on this occasion."Sorya says as he takes a quick gulp of the wine, shaking his head furiously as he did so. The wine must be sour.

"Have this,"I offer him water.

"I don't know Sorya. Should I drag her into my life? I hardly have the money to marry a woman like her. She can easily get a better person than me. She never saw my house. I seriously doubt if she is knowing what she is getting into."I say.

"What you say is of the least sense. Sorry to say that but if it was earlier I would be more open to you. Your act of suicide is constraining to give my opinion. Invite her to your home. I know you have nothing to hide from her. She is intelligent and would have already been through considering her life with you.

I remain silent pouring another glass of wine into my glass. I sip it and stare at Sorya.

"You want me to leave,"Sorya asks.

"For the first time, your advice has given more clarification than confusion. Let me invite her to my house."I say smiling at him.

" Good brother "Sorya laughs aloud.

"We are not going to sleep without finishing the wine today," He says.

"How can I invite her alone to my house?"

"You do not worry, we will extend the invite to my house for lunch or dinner. While leaving you can take her to your house,"Sorya says.

"Seems like you are good at drawing plans instantly,"I say.

"I am yet to plan for the future of my family in my absence,"Sorya says.

"Nothing will happen to you Sorya. We will need to go to the city again. Please do not say no to me, I think the doctor would give us a better detail of your health if Kala is not with you. Champa said so."

"If Champa said, so be it, we will go not for me but you, I hope it will give some private time for both of you to discuss. If she joins us, though."

"I think she will join, need to ask."

"Let me ask," Sorya says.

"No, you don't have to, I mean you don't have to request her to come for your health, it is our responsibility,"

"Go ahead brother, you can talk to her, I won't disturb you both,"He says pouting his lower lip at me.

"You are a crazy fellow,"I say smiling at him and waving my hand in disapproval of his remarks.

We finish the wine and Sorya heads back home. I do not remember when he left exactly, but I saw his silhouette merging with darkness in the middle of the night as he left.

The next day when I woke up, I see Champa standing in front staring at me. I wonder if Sorya already spoke to her and invited her as per our plan. Even in that case, it is not lunchtime yet, and she must be at Sorya's house.

"Was least expecting you"Please come inside I say

"No I cannot come inside, let us talk here," Champa says.

"What happened, "I ask

"The delay yesterday night and the people who gathered yesterday spoke to Yiey and made her believe that we are having an affair."

"I see that. I will talk to Yiey,"I say

"It is not that simple now, Yiey disowned me, she will get me married to someone very soon."

"Not to worry, I do not think she would do that at least at such a pace"

"She is resolute in finding someone by this month."
"How can she be so mean? she must understand your feeling." I say.
"Mean? Alright neither do you nor she understand me."
"She raised you, so she is trying to do this in haste, is she your paternal or maternal grandmother?"I ask.
"She raised me. I am an orphan. Unlike you she is not trying to leave me hastily. She is trying to fulfil her responsibility. She cares for me. I got my answer. Will leave"Champa says and rushes towards a cart from which she came, outside the gate.

"Champa Champa, wait,"I say.

I rush to wash my face with water and run after her. I grab her shoulder in front of everyone. The few people on the street stared at us. Champa feels irritated by my act and pushes me away. She walks faster to get into the cart and leaves.

I go to Sorya's house not knowing what is to be done. I did not want to follow her which would only cause her to despise me more.

"Sorya, Sorya"I bang on his door. With a slight creaking noise, the door opens wide and there is Sorya with his face bulged like a frog belly.

"You again? Come sleep, I have more wine do not tell the kids" says Sorya swaying at the door and mumbling something in a whisper.

"You are still in a hangover?"I ask.

"I am normal, fine, good,"he stutters crouching gradually at the door.

"I should have followed Champa and convinced her instead of coming for you."

"Okay meet me at our field when you are sober," I say. I know he may not have processed what I said, but his subconscious mind would have registered it.

I walk towards my field and all thoughts seem to rush within me. Am I wise or foolish? A person like me can never get a beautiful girl like Champa for a wife. On top of it, she is asking me to marry. I think I will have to go for her, come what may.

I walk straight to Yiey's house. On the way I think about her and worry about losing her, a few hours back I was stone cold and still like a rock but now I do not know how the fountain of love is rushing within me. I walk three times faster than my usual pace. There are fields on either side and stretches of greenery along the sides of the mud road. Yet I only see them, my thoughts are elsewhere.

"Champa, Champa,"I shout in front of her house.

"What do you want?"Yiey asks.

"Please call Champa I have to talk to her,"I say.

"She is not coming out, she is not going to meet you hereafter,"Yiey says.

"I just need to talk to her at once,"I say.

A broad face man with a wheatish skin tone, grabbing a moustache that looks like a caterpillar is watching me passively as I spoke to Yiey.

"Is he that one?" he asks Yiey

"Yes," Yiey says as she hands over a small packet of stuff concealed in a paper for which he paid her shortly.

"I will take care," He says to Yiey.

Yiey walks inside the house stepping down from the pod-shaped shop. I walk towards the entrance to open the door, but it seems to be locked. I knock on the door calling out to Champa.

"You want to talk to Champa," He asks.

"Yes, that is exactly what I want,"I say.

"Okay, come with me," He says.

I follow the person and walk along the mud road distancing much ahead of Champa's house. He moves into a small path crafted by human tracks along the barren field. After a few minutes of walking, we arrive at a hut which is elevated from the ground by four supporting shafts.

"Sit inside," He says.

"Where is Champa," I ask.

"She will be here in no time," He says.

I sense something is wrong and try reverting. The man grabs my shoulder and with brute force swirls me to the ground. I lay there shocked in the dust. I kick the left leg of the man standing in front of me. As he tilts, I punch him in the groin. He falls to the ground. In no time a couple of others join him and kick me while I lay on the ground. They kick and punch all over my body and face. Initially, I tried to resist and fight back, but I am overpowered by them. If I punch back, they will be infuriated and rage even more. I lay dead unconscious. The men walk away feeling a triumph out of their accomplished task.

I lay there for a solid hour gathering strength from every part of my body trying to recover from the imminent pain inflicted within me. I gain every bit of life out of my body and get up to slowly walk away from the place. I sway like a pendulum as I walk. I walk past Yiey's house which indicates I am in the right direction. I pass out and fall on the road. My breath is getting thinner. If I do not rise now, this will be my last moments of life. I look at the blue clouds and the green lush along the sides of the road which I ignored earlier, lying there, dying in peace.

CHAPTER SEVEN

2016 Singapore

Narrator: Arka

"Finally we made it," I say.

"Yeah, it was such a long queue."

"Good that we started early"

"My bad, I should not have planned for today. The long weekend is always like this."

"That's alright, the long weekend is when there are a lot of people and we can have the feeling of a tour though it is an official trip for you."

"I hope the client is happy with my property proposal and is willing to invest in it"

"So you are selling him what? A condo, mansion or an apartment?"

"In simple words, It is a business complex, which the client wanted to take over. He wanted to look into the financials and conclude if it is profitable to take over as is or demolish and construct for something else which is more profitable."

"Who is the client?"

"No offence, we have an NDA, Client confidentiality, so,"Tevy says.

"Oh that's fine, thanks."

Finally, after crossing the Johor-Singapore causeway, we enter Singapore.

"I have a friend in Singapore we can stay in his condo," I say.

"I have a surprise for you," Tevy says

"What is that?"

"We are going to stay at the Marina Bay Sands,"Tevy says.

"Wow! Your company is making a lot of money."

"No it is the client. They are hosting me for my stay here."

"Are you sure they won't mind me staying with you"

"They won't visit us at the hotel. I assume"

"I think I should better stay at my friend's place and visit you."

"No that should be okay, you can stay with me as long as you do not mind sharing the room."

"I still doubt the idea, though I am perfectly fine to share the room with you."

"Alright let's head on to the hotel."

I key in Marina Bay Sands into my phone GPS, and we head in that direction. I give the key to the valet and head into the lobby.

"Your booking reservation,"Asks the staff

Tevy picks up her mobile and after a couple of minutes of talking, we head to the elevator.

The 27th floor is where we are going to stay. We provide the security card at multiple points and finally head to the room lit in amber lights with a panoramic window seamlessly blending into the sky above, the tranquillity of the sea visible behind the towering structures of lights and gardens underneath.

"I will have a walk around," I say,

"You don't want to fresh up"

"I am as fresh as a green apple just plucked from a tree."

"Alright, go ahead I will take a shower."

I pick up the access card and walk towards the elevator reaching the 57th floor. There are some pubs and outlets on the open roof and an Infinity pool. Walking along the stretch at the pool there are sunloungers and floating pods. After a short walk along the length of the rooftop, I get back to the room.

I tap the security card and walk in. Tevy is on a call with someone.

"Is everything ready? What? What is the problem? Are you kidding me? " Tevy talks on her phone

As I near her she looks at me and abruptly disconnects the call.

"What happened?"

"Nothing, the deal seems to have been awarded to someone else"

"So?" I shrug at Tevy

"Even I am confused. They could have updated us ahead."

"We may have to check out,"Tevy says.

"No let it be, I liked the place I will take care of the expenses," I say.

"No! I cannot accept that. My friend has arranged her condo for us to stay, she is overseas and it is available to occupy since we already checked in we can continue to stay for today and can leave tomorrow."

"Great we can roam around Singapore then,"

"I have two more small clients who I was referring due to travel for a while, I will complete that in another two days from tomorrow post that we can hang around."

"Okay with me, I got my camera and lenses, not to worry," I say.

"Let us go to the city and have lunch,"Tevy says.

After an hour of back and forth, I pick my 17-24 f2.8 Canon lens and my 5D camera over my 35mm prime for a better range. We go towards the MRT station nearby and take the red line towards City Hall. We step outside and walk towards the peninsular plaza which I am aware is a good place for used camera purchases and repair. We roam around randomly at the place until it is almost evening. We have laksa at a food court in the plaza. We finish lunch and again go towards stores of camera gear.

"Wow," I say staring at one of the displays in the shop.
"What is it?" Tevy asks,
"So many 35mm film cameras, Leica M, Contax, and many more"
"Let me buy some film,"I say.

We walk into Ruby photo studio shop nearby and I purchase a twelve-pack 35 mm roll of Kodak. I pick my Yashica Electro 35 from the bag and load it with the film. Immediately Tevy poses at me in her flower pattern jumpsuit and I snap her pose.

"So how is it?"She asks.
"Great"
"No preview yet right,"She asks.
"I know it is great, as long as nothing is messed up in the post-production of the roll,"I say smiling.

We walk ahead from the Plaza reaching the Singapore Parliament building which is more like a Palace with no guards. There is only a small glass counter. Most of the area is covered by Surveillance. Besides, that is Clarke Quay which is synonymous with drinks, dance and fun. We sit for a while near the Botero bird facing the river watching the boats gliding along on the water bed in wood boats. After a couple of minutes, we walk along to the bridge connecting to the pubs. The beats of the dance pubs are reverberating until the place we sat on the bridge. A teen lady busker gets an Epiphone guitar and begins to play Hotel California followed by Stairway to Heaven. It was good vibes but her tunes are overpowered by the dance beats arising from the pubs. You can switch your focus to either of them, which needs some practice and is easier with some alcohol intake, which does not help focus on what you need but helps to ignore the beat you wish to.

"Do you like to have some vodka?"I ask.

"I am not sure," Tevy says.

Shortly, a dance group arrives that does some Hawaii folk dance steps. The beat goes wild, and the vibe is really good.

"Let's get the vodka,"Tevy says.

We place the bottle of Vodka on the bridge and pour ourselves small sips each. We join the crowd watching the performance but unlike others, we start to dance to the drum beats. Tevy goes wild, I jump randomly with some structure of dance in between. Soon the crowd goes frenzy and are no longer mute spectators. This goes on for an hour, me or Tevy taking short breaks to refill our plastic glasses with vodka.

Towards the end of the street performance, a folk song is sung followed by the crowd cheer to conclude.

Tevy jumps onto the sitting area on the bridge only to fail and fall back. I hold her hip and give a gentle lift helping her to land on the sitting area. When it was my turn, I make two attempts to finally land beside her. Tevy lays flat on her back looking at the sky.

"I love this," She says.

"What ?"I ask.

"Look at the stars"

"I see only clouds,"I say.

"Look closer," She says and grabs my shoulder making me lay on my back beside her.

As I observe, each star in the sky starts to shine bright. It was right in front of me, yet I could not notice at first instance. The closer I focus more stars are revealed.

"Absolutely Brilliant," I say.

"Do you know how long they are there?"Tevy asks.

"Millions of years could be, I wish I knew,"

"Do you think they were there before the vodka is found?"

"Yes"

"Before dance?"

"Yes"

"Before love?"

"I think they are there before human existence, love is later to it,"

"I think love existed before humans arrived on Earth."

"You mean the plants and trees loved each other?"

"I do not know, but I feel love was always there, the sky, the wind, the sea, they love each other,"Tevy says.

"I need to be sober to decipher that,"I say.

"So what's next?"

"I don't know maybe to finish our vodka or take it to our hotel."

"I want another sip of it, but I am hungry."

"Let us go to boat quay then just a few metres away and there are a lot of restaurants lined up for us to have food."

"Alright"

We walk to a nearby seafood restaurant, have dinner in the moonlight by the Singapore River and walk towards the road to catch a taxi after some long waiting and the multiple deny requests in booking apps we finally get a car and reach the hotel. Both of us are quite drunk, and Tevy is seriously on a high. She barely knew we was in our room and mumbling something about getting a grab car to reach the hotel. I take her to the restroom and wash her face with water and place her on the bed. There is still some unfinished vodka in my bag which I open and mix with orange juice in the fridge and sip it.

"Come here,"Tevy says.

"Wait," I grunt and walk towards her.

"Open that blue bag near the TV console," She says authoritatively.

"I walk there and open it,"I dislike her tone yet I think it is the work of alcohol on her.

"Pick the blue nightgown," She says.

I run my hand through the clothes and pick a blue silk nightgown.

"Pass it on, "She says.

I throw the nightwear at her.

"Thanks, face the wall until I say further."

"Turn," She says after a minute or two.

I notice her nipples popping out on the silk and her breasts protruding over her dress more than usual. I walk back to my chair and sit there at the panoramic view of the gardens.

"Are the gardens beautiful?"She asks.

"Yes but dimly lit now so not much is visible"

"Are they more attractive than me? I am well lit by the way."

"You are always attractive" I look at her and say with a serious expression on my face. Somehow I am not comfortable with this conversation.

"You want to sleep over beside me."

"No I am good here, I don’t really need a bed."

"Are you thinking of someone else?"Tevy asks.

"No, I am not thinking anything at all."

"Alright you can sleep over beside me if you want,"Tevy says.

I was puzzled Tevy never spoke like this, it could be the alcohol or she is actually being nicer to me with no intentions. It could be that I am thinking more than I should.

I sleep on the sofa and about 5 AM I wake up to see Tevy asleep hugging the pillow like a baby. I take a piss and move my sofa towards the TV and watch the Formula One highlights of last year.

"So early,"Tevy asks in a coarse voice which is still tuning itself out of sleep.

"Ya," I say.

She continues to sleep with no response.

At 7 AM, I sleep on the other side of the bed after waking up from the sofa.

"Wake Up," Tevy says.

"Had your breakfast?"I ask.

"Not yet, you are sleeping for the past two hours I did not want to wake you up," Tevy says.

"Oh Sorry, what time is our checkout?"I ask.

"11 AM,"Tevy says.

"Give me a few minutes I will be ready and we can leave,"I say.

We pick up our car from the valet and check out of the hotel.

"Where are we going now?"I ask.

"To the condo of my friend in Yew Tee," Tevy says.

Tevy key in the pin code and we drive straight to the national highway and then connect to the service road. This place is very quiet, unlike the city. I could immediately feel it much better than the grandeur and hustle and bustle of the tourist spot we stayed at.

The security keys in our car number ask for the flat and floor number.

"Tenth Floor, 5th Unit," she says.

After some fiddling with the keys we finally manage to walk in, the hall is quite big and the rooms are very spacious with large beds and panoramic windows open to the road with a beautiful view.

"I will go to get some bread, and milk from FairPrice at Yew Tee Point, take rest, "Tevy says to me.

"I will join you,"I say.

"No that's okay"I need a walk tired of pushing the pedal.

I walk into the hall and lie on the sofa with the remote in my hand, as Tevy leaves for errands. I turn on the TV and click on the Netflix button on my remote when it asks for some credentials. I enter and then pause on the search field for a while. I scroll down the suggestions for crime thrillers.

I hear the phone ring. I guess Tevy left the phone at the house. I walk into the room and press the volume button to silence it. I could see Tevy crossing the signal from the view of my window. Her hair jumps on her back like a pony as she walks on her heels. With her business outfit, she looks very desirable. I find her very attractive these days. Sometimes when she walks, it is almost like Nila. Only Tevy has a clear mind, unlike Nila whose thoughts are webbed like Spaghetti and I am no fork to segregate and comprehend them.

I walk back to the hall and see a trailer of some Anime running as I last hovered the select on it. I hear some sound in the kitchen and walk towards there only to notice that the sound is from the Kitchen of the neighbour's house. There are utility balconies and space separating the two kitchens.

"Seems like new tenants," shouts the teen girl in the kitchen at the neighbour's house walking towards her mother as she glances at me.

I make no efforts to correct or covey them as I am tired and wanted to take some rest. I keep running along with the catalogue of crime movies and finally settle on an Anime of Van Helsing. In the fridge there are a couple of beers, I pick a Carlsberg while making a note to replenish the stock when we move out.

I notice some magazines placed under the desk of the teapoy in the hall. I pull out to see that most of the content is sexual. There are pictures of nude women in between magazines. I run through the pages and place them back with not much interest. I am not particularly interested in nudity unless I have not masturbated in a while. There are some fiction novels on the rack, fortunately, they are not like the magazines, but most of them are good collections of history and teen fiction.

There is a knife set beside the TV along with pictures of some women, I take it and place it in the kitchen. It looks like I have seen her before, a familiar face. I place the photos in the drawer in the TV console.

I rest for a while on the couch hearing to the action sequences of the Anime without watching it. As it bothers me rest I turn it off. I wake up to the smell of chicken curry cooked in the kitchen. I walk over to see Tevy cooking.

"Woke up ?"Yes, I say.

"I thought you would have some more rest,"I say.

"I could not sleep as it is a new place, I usually have this problem."

"I had a sound sleep."

"Ya I heard you snoring, very sound," She smiles at me.

"That is gross, I should have taken caution."

"That is fine, you don't have to shy away from me, we like each other."
"Do we?"
Tevy smiles and stirs the chicken curry. I feel good at that.
"I am more hungry after smelling your food."
"15 minutes more"
"I will have a shower by then."
"Okay"

After a shower, I clear the dining table of stuff and place them in the right order. I run the vacuum on the floor and the curtains.

"Food is ready," Tevy says.
"Delicious, this pasta is so unique with those herbs, I like it"
"Secret herbs, I forgot to get some beer,"Tevy says.
"I had that covered,"I say as I walk along to the refrigerator and get two more cans of it, making a count of three in my mind.
"Great! We need to refill them."
"I am tracking them. We will."
"Tracking? You had already."
"Yup I had one"
"Nowonder you snored so hard,"Tevy laughs
"Let me focus on my food" I dismiss her and continue to relish the taste.
"I need to go to the office tomorrow,"Tevy says.
"Okay, I will walk around the city then."
"Save some locations to visit with me."
"I will pick the best ones for you," I say.
"Thank you."
"No cooking tomorrow, let's have dinner elsewhere"
"Which means you did not like my food"
"No not at all, I wanted you to have a break."
"I know, just kidding,"

We finish lunch and get ourselves into shorts and tees with a cap on me and a straw hat for Tevy.

"This time I will drive," I say to Tevy.

"Alright."

The four-cylinder Chevy was lagging power on the highway but it seemed to be good for the city with its low-end torque. We drive randomly until we reach Little India. It seemed to be the only place in Singapore where there are more violations of traffic rules. People seem to jaywalk on the road. There are small streets in which to manoeuvre. We look to park the car at the Mustafa Centre and walk towards SimLim Square. There are many food courts on the way for which Singapore is famous. We walk into the Indian Heritage Center. After some random surfing on the information, we walk towards MRT to go to Chinatown. Tevy buys a selfie stick there, and I get some memory cards for my Fujifilm xt100 for backup. The place is colourful and there are a lot of items you can buy for under fifty dollars. Almost every shop in the lane has a Singapore souvenir. I hesitantly posed for selfies with Tevy as she is insisting very much on it at the end of every street. I am a photographer who does not like to be photographed. At this point in time, I do not want to say it to Tevy and spoil the otherwise pleasant day.

We go to Harbourfront from there and walk over to the terrace top wading pool. After watching the fireworks, we take the travelator along the boardwalk and reach Sentosa Island.

"Shall we go to the casino?"Tevy asks.

"Okay"

We deposit our bags and enter the casino, we keep hopping tables raising our minimum bet once in a while at roulette. After losing two hundred dollars we find the dice game and spend thirty minutes losing and gaining small amounts. We bet on the banker for Bacarrat and win three hundred gaining a hundred.

"Let's go,"I say.

"I think we can win more,"Tevy says.

"Lend me your hundred. I will play for you."

I pass on the chips worth a hundred to her. In ten seconds, the hundred is gone in a simple card game.

We walk out of the casino. I will transfer you my hundred tell me your bank details.

"That's okay," I say.

"No, I need your account number, so I can transfer,"Tevy says,

"I did not come to the casino to invest money at least. It was the fun we had over there,"I say,

"Really, I thought you were bored."

"I was not, I was just curious which led to a serious expression,"I say,

"I defer believing it, though I know that money is not your concern but something else."

"Ya I was wondering if we had played poker instead of the games which are purely based on luck,"I say.

"So your chances of winning at poker are good?"Tevy says.

"Probably, there is some talent needed in poker along with luck,"I say,

"Well I knew something new about you in that case."

"What is that?"I ask.

"You can put up a face which may not be what you feel,"Tevy says.

"What nonsense, "I say.

"Excuse me !!"Tevy shrieks

"Why are you yelling now, how can you pass judgement on me?I say.

"No, I was just saying since you said you were good at poker,"Tevy says.

"I am good at a game does not mean I fake my expressions,"I say.

"I did not say you faked expressions, I just said that you may not reveal."

"I know what you meant,"I say.

"Never mind, I just got to see some real feelings out of you,"Tevy says.

"What? Forget it, please leave, I do not want to waste time arguing with someone who has no capability to understand," I say.

I stop a taxi and open the door as Tevy get in I close the door and wave goodbye at her. I rapidly walk down the steps of the bridge we were talking at, I needed to be alone after the altercation. After a couple of minutes, I walk above the bridge to see that there is no sign of the taxi or Tevy. I walk along the highway pavement with lights flooding the road in orange. I pick my camera and shoot pictures of the landscape along the way. It was just two minutes of discussion which led to a rift between us for the first time. Maybe I was wrong everyone has a Nila in them or maybe I am exaggerating the discussion to that point. This could be normal between couples. Sending the partner in a Cab at night, alone ? may not be. I know Singapore is a very safe country yet I am not sure if that makes me immune to the after-effects of the incident with Tevy. I place my camera on a boundary wall to shoot a long exposure of the bridge while capturing the stars.F22 seems the suitable setting of aperture for it. I press the shutter cable and wait for a few minutes to release it. After three attempts I get the perfect shot. I walk over further killing two hours from when Tevy left. It is 3 AM now. There is no call from Tevy on my phone, either she did not save my number or did not wish to call me. I did not save her number. I walk towards a restaurant and order a pint.

I ask for another pint. Felt something chunky in my jacket, and I pull it out to find the keys to the Chevy car. I install the grab car app and booked to Mustafa Centre. It took me twenty minutes to get the car out of the parking lot. This place is busy 24*7. I drive back to the condo which was saved as "home" in GPS while coming. I enter the condo and press the doorbell but no response. I do it twice and thrice. The door opposite me opens, and an old woman is watching me. I am not sure if Tevy is intentionally not opening the door or if she is not inside. I do not see her footwear outside I open the shoe rack there are ladies' sandals but I cannot recollect what Tevy was wearing today. I dial in her number but no response. The lady granny from the opposite house is still watching me. She is very curious. I can only feel that she is watching, yet I do not look at her directly. I cannot take it anymore I stare at her directly and she closes the door immediately. She is just curious but not brave to confront me. I take the lift looking at the finishing of the buttons and the mirrors as it glides down. I walk towards the swimming pool which is now not lit, and the fountain is shut down. In a dimly lit area, I sit. I feel like smoking a cigarette. I definitely cannot sleep here. I see some lights on the roof of the car park. I walk over to the condo route map on one of the posts mounted near the garden to find that there is a wading pool and BBQ pits on the rooftop of the multi-level car park. I walk over to the building and walk towards the pits. The place is empty with no one over there. I find a perfect bench to sleep on.

"Get up," says Tevy gently shaking me to wake me up.
"You,"I say and crouch on the bench to sit.

"How long have you been here? I ask.
"I came just now, was searching for you,"
"Where did you go last night?
"I slept at my friend's place."
"Okay"
"You slept here all night."
"Yes, I did not have the keys."
"Keys were in the shoe placed in the shoe rack, I think you know that."
"How am I supposed to know that?"I speak softly pacing myself away from her since I did not brush my teeth yet.
"Okay my bad should have told you,"
"You did not answer my call either."
"Did not check it later, ringtone was low maybe"
"Let's go,"Tevy says.

I point my finger at the sky towards the dramatic clouds diffusing the orange light of the rising sun and the blue light of the night sky.

"Wonderful," Tevy says as she sits beside me watching the sunrise.

She sits closer to me as I gently tug her. We close our eyes and sleep for the next fifteen minutes over there. After a while, the morning sun gets brighter, so we get up and walk towards the unit. Tevy opens the door, and I walk straight to the sofa and fall on it, Tevy joins me. We hug and sleep for about an hour. After this, Tevy abruptly wakes up and goes inside the room. I try to bother less about it and continue to sleep. I wake up in thirty minutes and brush my teeth. Tevy is toasting bread with egg for breakfast. She packs her breakfast and leaves some for me on the table.

"I am going to meet the client,"Tevy says as she rushes towards the door in her formal pinstriped suit, white shirt and heels.

"Okay, I place the key in the shoe if I go out ?"
"Yes, though I prefer you pick up my call so I can join you outside in case I am late."
"Okay I will, you were the defaulter yesterday,"I say to her softly with a sarcastic smile.
"Tevy," I say.
"Yes, tell me I am running out of time."
"You look good," I say.
"Is it my dress?"
"No, it is you."
I walk over to her and stare into her eyes, with a mix of feelings we look at each other. I do not know who started, but we kiss passionately on the lips. I am having arousal now. I try to unbutton her shirt.

"No, No not here, not now,"Tevy says as she withdraws herself from me. She kisses me one more time irresistibly and so does I as she finally withdraws herself and leaves in a hurry.

I watch TV do some callisthenics and check my equity account statement received in my email. I also see emails of rental deposits done into my account from my property in India. I publish my phone number to all of them so that they revert me later. I am no longer living in a stone cave, I smile at myself. After four hours I am pretty much aware of each and every feature of my phone and every minute detail of the TV remote. I feel that Tevy is not going to come until the evening, so I decide to go out.

"Salmon fish with fries," I say at the Long John Silver's food counter in Yew Tee point.
"Dine in or Takeaway."
"Dine in."
"Please take this and be seated, we will call you," says the teen at the counter

I place the number 24 on the table and keep waiting for their call. Meanwhile, I pick up my phone to see anything interesting in my Facebook account which I recently created. I have gone from zero usages to high screen usage in a very short time. I did not upload my picture nor did I indicate my name correctly in my account. I am still sceptical to do. I did use Orkut a long time back in the internet café but this is something yet new to me. I just look into random friends' suggestions provided to me.

"Tevy, Tevy!! " I gently shout coming to my senses that the glass partition in between us is a sound barrier.

I rush to open the glass door and walk towards her.

"Hey!!"You are here.

"Yes, I came to have lunch."

"Come."

We walk towards my table.

"What shall I order for you?"

"Anything is fine, something light," Tevy says.

"Salmon fish? Same as mine"

"Okay without the fries"

"Got it"

"So how did it turn out, client," I ask.

"They were a sweet couple. They are very happy with my presence, I think the deal is going to close positively."

"Good so you do have some purpose for the visit now"

"True, I was slightly upset when the major proposal got backed out but this is good."

"Shall we marry?"Tevy asks out of the blue.

"What?"I was completely taken aback by that statement.

"Forget it," She says.

"I mean."

"Forget it, I was just teasing you," She says interrupting me.

We finish lunch silently.

I ponder on her last question. Did she really mean it? We walk silently towards the MRT. Neither of us knows how to come up with a conversation after what she just asked.

"Should we marry?" I ask her.

"I said I was teasing you," She says.

When is your next appointment I ask? Nothing for today. Where shall we go?

"Let's go anywhere we want,"Tevy says.

"Didn't get you"

"Pick a place on the MRT map, and we go there."

"Sounds like too much of a plan"

Tevy laughs at me. We pick the map from the MRT counter and headed to take the train which first arrived on the right side of the platform.

"Chinatown," Tevy says.

"That does not sound like a random pick," I say.

"No questions please"

"Alright, let's go."

"What's that?"

"My camera"

"Looks smaller"

"Mirrorless, I prefer street photography sometimes"

"Today I will shoot,"Tevy says stretching her hand for me to give the camera.

"It's all yours"I pass on.

We alight in Chinatown.

"That one?" what is it called,

"Looks like a temple"

"Tooth Relic temple,"I say looking at my GPS.

Incense candles are burnt outside the temple. Small buddhas are intricately placed on the walls and gold glitter the place all over. While the entrance seemed like any usual temple it gradually ravelled into a sizeable hall with profound details over large walls.

"Where is the relic?Tevy asks.

"What relic?"

"Tooth relic"

"I don't know."

"Upstairs"

"There is a controversy surrounding the relic, some say it is not of Buddha"

"Is it?

"Yes but the abbot has denied it."

"Even Midas would run off out of gold to put into this design"

"Yes, I wonder how far a belief system can take you"

Tattoo shops, Electronics, and Food, very busy streets indeed. Almost everyone on the street has a hat and a camera. Very few flats were spotted nearby in the commercial complex. We walk over to the MRT after an hour of playing Maze on the streets. I grab a Gatorade to drink.

"Throw it,"Tevy says.

"Why?"

"You cannot drink inside the MRT"

"I can carry it, don't have to throw it."

"Alright"

We take the MRT skipping and switching lines until we reach Promenade. What is special about this place I ask her. This is the Suntec City Convention the one-stop for all kinds of gadgets on sale. They have different themes of electronics on specified dates. I have checked out this place on my mobile today there is also the largest fountain in the world nearby.

"Fountain of wealth, "I say,

"How do you know it?

"I saw it on the map in the MRT"

We walk around in circles in the convention centre, TV units are sold on limited sale. There is a salesman at every counter, and some of them are screaming at the pitch of their voice to attract consumers with features of the products.

I get a GPS for my motorcycle, and Tevy gets a power bank and a wireless Beats headset. There is a diverse display of laptops in the basement from lowest to the highest spec.

The fountain of wealth doesn't actually feel like the world's tallest unless you take the staircase to walk along with the height of it only a portion of it is visible at the ground level. I was amused by the way it is concealed underneath surrounded by outlets and food joints. The water sprouting from the fountain dances in synchrony with the beats of the music and is an enthralling experience.

We walk over to the street level and wait to cross the road or take a taxi.

"How do I connect this ?"Tevy asks.

"There should be a Bluetooth button, find it."

"I did but it is not activated by press."

"Long press"

"Okay, got it, paired"

Tevy moves her head in rhythm to the song she is listening to. Tevy notices the road empty ahead of her and a pickup Van halted on her right. She takes a sudden jump from the pavement and jogs to cross the road. I follow her behind. A speeding biker slams right into Tevy in her groin and he skids along the road the bike loses control and rams onto the leg of Tevy falling on the bed of plants separating the road. I missed the crash a few inches behind and shouted aloud in shock. The crowd yells at once at the sudden occurrence and runs towards us. The biker is fully equipped with his riding gear and did not suffer any major injury, yet he seems to be disappointed at the occurrence as he waves his head in disapproval of Tevy. Tevy is holding her groin and screaming in pain. I run towards Tevy.

"Tevy!! Are you bleeding? what happened?"I ask while Tevy continues to shriek.

I check her foot and notice she is bleeding from the ankles which got abraded by the road. She is holding her groin and I also suspect internal injuries.

"The ambulance will be here shortly," says a man probably in his seventies with a silver beard and a Taqiyah on his head.

I understand that I am in a state of panic as well and my hand is trembling uncontrollably.

"It's Okay, It's okay, You will be fine" I hug Tevy and cry as she continues to be in agony, screaming. I am very worried at this point.

In ten minutes we could hear the ambulance approaching us. The Biker who was earlier furious and talking to himself and the few people beside him against the audacious crossing of the road by Tevy has calmed himself and approached us as he sees Tevy in pain.

"Are you okay?"He asks.

Tevy waves her hand with is not indicative of anything. Maybe she is conscious is what she wants to convey.

As we approach the ambulance, I help place Tevy on the stretcher in the rear. I quickly rush to the biker.

"Please take down my number. I will cover the damages to your bike,"I say.

"That's okay, please take care of her,"He says as he gently pats my shoulder indicating I get into the ambulance.

"Thank You,"I say to him folding both my hands in a namaste, grateful.

The ambulance accelerates like a stone released from the straps of a catapult. I lost track of time in spite of the speeding vehicle I can feel every second of time uncompromising and duly finish its duration. The drag of time is annoying. A minute seems forever. We finally reach the Accident and Emergency wing of Singapore General Hospital. Tevy is rushed into the ICU after some examination by the doctor at this point, Tevy is still unconscious.

Nurses are rushing to the ICU where Tevy is admitted. I was told to wait outside. I was asked for my name and identification for me and Tevy.No other formalities are asked at this point in time. Another male nurse asks me for details of the incident which he jots down briefly in his notepad and walks towards the Doctor attending Tevy.

"Does this belong to you?" An attendant walks over to me and asks giving me the handbag of Tevy and the newly purchased headphones scraped off the black matt paint over it due to the accident.

"Yes," I say

It suddenly occurs to me that Tevy had a head injury after seeing the earphones. I rush towards the ICU.

"Doctor! Doctor," I shout.

An attendant comes over.

"Yes"

"I think she may have had a head injury."

"She did have, there is no bleeding though however, we suspect an internal impact to the head. An MRI will be done, did you have any injuries,"The doctor asks me.

"No Doctor I am fine," I say.

"Okay, please be seated, will call for you as needed,"He says.

"What is her condition now"
"She is still unconscious, we cannot report anything until the scan reports are obtained,"The doctor says.

After an hour of waiting. I feel hungry and walk over to the vending machine and buy a coffee.

"She had multiple fractures and is still unconscious," The doctor says to me as he approaches.
"We suppose she is in a coma state. Her eyes are open and she is able to hear us but there is no voluntary action from her."
"Will she be back to normal doctor ?"
"She has a ten per cent chance which is a lot of chance for these conditions, you can talk to her, in a way it can improve her activation of the brain."

I drop my coffee in the bin and sanitize my hands as directed by the Nurse and wear an apron. I walk inside the ICU and sit beside Tevy on an iron stool.

"It happened so quickly, do not do this Tevy, please wake up, I wish I delayed giving your headphone or I held your hand,"I say with tears filled in both eyes as I see Tevy lying on the bed lifeless, pipes and wires connected to her nostrils. It is gut-wrenching to see her like that. I slept beside her bed losing track of time.

I wake up at 3 AM at night and look at Tevy.

"I want to marry you Tevy, yes I want to, please come back I need you."

The nurse enters the room.

"What does she eat doctor?"

"She will be fed slurry with the tube."

"Will she recover Nurse?"

"Never lose your hope. She will."

"Thank you, yes, she will,"I say.

"Can you help me lift her?"

"Sure"

I lift Tevy to 90 degrees on her bed reclining slightly.

"Are you married to her?"

"No"

"You can leave now, I will need to take care of her routine."

"Okay," I said and walked out of the room.

"Can I be back in,"

"30 minutes" reply the Nurse pouncing upon my question.

I take the elevator and walk straight to the main road. I buy a pack of Marlboro and an orange juice Tetra pack.

I walk farther until the bus stop. The air is warm outside. I lit my cigarette standing beside the bin. What is this? Why? I am still unable to ingest this situation into my mind and accept that it happened. It was so quick. I need to collect Tevy's things from her friend's condo. I may also have to inform them. I do not have any of Tevy's contact with me nor do I know unlock code of her phone. I do not know when that phone will be unlocked or if it would be ever. Her life went from everything to 10% due to an incident in a matter of a few seconds. The life which we cling to so hard is so fragile. A single mistake and we are on the verge of a crisis. All these thoughts flood my mind. Yet I do not give up on the negative consequences, I believe she will recover.

Before I felt anything from the cigarette it was already done. I drop it into the bin and light another indulging back in the same thoughts which began when I lit the first cigarette. At the completion of a third one, I give up and walk over to the hospital sipping on the drink to avoid any bad breath from the cigarette. Someone is walking behind me as I turn around he, takes a different line and moves towards the car park. Is he confused like me or is he following me? I felt the same in Yew Tee when I was having lunch. I walk towards the reception and fetch a newspaper from the rack and sit on the sofa, opposite me is a mirror. I watch him walk towards the car park for a few more steps. At this point, he turns towards the sofa on which I am sitting separating from him by a glass. He is walking towards me I could see it in the mirror opposite to me, I do not think he figured out that I am watching him. I turn my head to watch him. In a panic, he starts jogging towards the bus stop. I walk towards the door and run after him. He runs faster. There is a guy waiting on a bike ahead of the stop where I was smoking. He gets onto the bike and jerks the shoulder of the driver alerting him to accelerate. He escapes two feet ahead of me.

I sit on the bench at the bus stop. Who are these guys following me? Did they follow me or was he just curious? No, he definitely followed me.

I walk towards the hospital, and the lady at the reception is waving at me.

"Are you the attendant of Tevy Sir? "She asks.

"Yes"

"Please sign here, check the name FIN and other details"

"Okay"

I walk towards the elevator and forgot the floor number. I re-check at the reception and pressed four.

"Can I come in?" I ask.

"Yes"

After a few minutes, the nurse leaves the room.

"Please inform her kin about the situation," she says as she leaves.

I am not sure about Tevy's particulars, her company or her family. I think deeply for a minute about how to inform them. After a couple of minutes, I give up and doze in the chair until morning.

At 7 AM in the morning.

"Excuse me," says someone at the door.

"Hi"

"I am Priya Tevy's friend."

"What happened to her"

"She met with an accident while crossing the road."

"How could she?"

"How do you know Tevy?"

"You stayed at my condo."

"Oh Alright"

"She was crossing the road and did not notice the biker."

"Were you not with her?

"I was behind her."

She walks over to Tevy holds her hand presses it hard. Place another hand on her forehead and sweeps backwards onto the hair.

"Okay, I got your clothes and other stuff from home."

"Thank you very much, I was actually thinking to reach your home and collect the stuff."

"Where do you eat?"

"I did not think of it yet. I did have a burger from the vending machine, there is also a food court nearby."

"Can I have a moment alone?" Priya asks.

"Sure," I say as I walk out of the room.

I walk past the bus stop towards a local Chinese store and buy a brush and toothpaste. I enter the hospital to walk towards the washroom and complete my routine.

After 45 minutes I re-enter Tevy's room.

"There is something on her lips,"I say to Priya

"Ya I fed her some Juice and cookies," Priya says.

"I am leaving,"Priya says after a couple of minutes.
"Okay, You know any relatives of Tevy,"I ask.
"Not very sure, I need to dig in. I will be back in two hours."
"Okay," I say.

The Nurse comes over in some time and takes some medical readings.

"Everything seems normal, we may need to take another MRI," says the head nurse as she leaves.

I look at Tevy she feels so alive. I lift the blanket of Tevy. I unravel her robe near the leg and look at her bruises. They are still healing.

There is a juicer and a few apples. I make a glass of juice, and place the straw in her mouth but she doesn't seem to sip in. I wonder how Priya fed Tevy.

"We will need to take an MRI to her tomorrow morning at 10 AM," the Nurse informed me standing outside the door.

I spend the night dreaming about all the days in Malaysia when I was alone and had nothing to do with anyone. Now I am here thinking of when Tevy wakes up. At this point in time, I do not know when Tevy would recover.

CHAPTER EIGHT

1971 – 1976 KAMPUCHEA (CAMBODIA)

Narrator: Heng Chann

I tend to my wounds in my hut, alive and breathing. Every inch of me is burning with disgust, contempt and hate for not being able to fight for myself. I stared at the doors of my hut for a week. I did not see anyone. I hid at the river behind my hut during the day, tending to my wounds and thinking about the insult. All the while I was not thinking about Champa but those scoundrels who inflicted pain upon me like rabid dogs. I gained my strength later during that day and walked in the night with torn clothes and my blood clotted by the cold night. My body is still sore though my wounds have healed.

"Are you there?" Sorya asks banging on the door.

I walk slowly towards the door and open it.

"Where have you been? I was searching everywhere for you,"Sorya says.

"I went to the neighbouring village."

"Why?"
"Heard someone know about my parents"
"Really!! Did you get to know anything?
"No", I conveniently lie to Sorya
"Forget it,"
"We are going to the city tomorrow,"Sorya says.
I nod my head in approval.
"Had your food?"
"Yes"
"I see the vessels clean."
"I washed them already."
"Okay,"
"I think you are worried about your parents. Okay take your time. I will see you tomorrow" Sorya says as he leaves.

The following day Surya and I start our journey to the city.

"What is it?"I ask.
"What?"He says.
"Why were you so keen today?"
"I got a plan, will tell you."
"Plan for what?"
"To earn money"
"Not to worry," I say.

I want to go back and talk to Champa, but I am embarrassed to speak up about whatever has happened to me.

"I want to go back," I say.
"What? No, we have to go to the city today,"
"Reveal your plan or we leave,"I say.
"We will start a business to get plastic items from the city and sell them in our village."
"But"
"I know what is on your mind, Champa and Yiey are already

doing it but did you ever notice the long queue outside their shop, the waiting is more, they are unable to meet the demand. Sometimes people wait for a week for orders to be fulfilled."

I think for a while, Sorya's words started to make some sense to me.

I wanted to avenge whatever happened, and Sorya's plan is the best way to do it.

"My intention is not to beat their business or hit on them. I wanted to fill the gap they are unable to cater to."

"I want to hit on their business," I say.

"What? Is it you speaking about Champa? You think she will like you for doing this?"

"I will handle her,"I say.

We walk towards a building in the city more like a shabby odd complex, ready to crumble any time.

"Are you sure it is here?"I ask.

We wait at the parking for another then minutes. The insects which gathered around the unevenly lit halogen lights seemed to be busier than us. They live for a day, yet they are hyperactive. The lizard on the wall is seizing on every opportunity to hunt and relish the insects.

"Hello gentlemen, how long are you here?" says an old man with a silk shirt, pink shade glasses, gold trim frame and layered gold chains.

"Quite some time, forty minutes," Sorya says.

"I waited for twenty-four hours to get my hands into this line of business in the early days," He says.

"Tell me, what do you want to do?"

"We want to sell plastics and household stuff."

"Boring," He says.

"We decided to go for it,"

"I thought you were clever, a week and you finally decided this?"He says.

"Anyway since you have decided, I will take you to my warehouse"

We follow him through a series of empty streets lit with neon lights. Women standing on either side of these streets walk into the light as men approach them. They walk to the nearby hotel if the deal is made else they revert to the shadows behind the light again.

We approach a closed shutter.

"Open," he says as he bangs on the door. The shutter is opened by a lady. I see her legs through the slit in the shutter.

"How many," She asks.

"Only three of us"

"You know all of them?"

"Yes, I do."

The shutter is fully opened.

We follow straight as she leads us to another warehouse from inside.

"Wait," He says.

"Not for that," She asks.

"No, they are new to the business and not aware of dealing with it," He says.

"She is not happy, you always give excuses," She says.

"I need time. You do your work, do not over-smart me,"He says.

"Talk carefully or there are many to replace your position"

"Okay, now walk me to the yellow box."

We walk farther down, post the exit of the warehouse towards a field passing a nearby lake. We get onto a boat and she rows to the other side. There is another warehouse.

"Here your go"

"We pick the ones we need?"Sorya asks.

"No picking, I will give you and you should sell them. You deliver promptly, you sell more, you fail, and this will be our last meeting," She says.

"By when should we sell?" I ask.

"Fourteen days, you sell whatever stuff you can and come here to report the earnings"

"Fourteen days is too short," Sorya says.

"Twenty days," She says.

That marks the beginning of our first pact in trade. We return home thinking of how to sell the stuff and live up to the promise. Sorya stays at my home and we hardly sleep that night. While Sorya is thinking of the new business. My mind is lingering over the past.

Sorya loads his cart with all the stuff we brought and drives to my place the next day before I wake up.

"We do not wait for them,"He says.

"No store"

"No need, we go to each house and sell what they need, "He says.

"Good Idea, "I say.

Initially, we drive the cart for two kilometres but no one is quite interested. There were busy with their lives. As the day breaks in some of them invite us hesitatingly into their porch and look at our stuff. Even in the fields, people get crazy buying stuff with plenty of time to look into the combs, plastic watches and leather belts. The ladies started to buy with freedom as their husbands worked in the fields. In two days, we sold all the stuff.

We load our carts twice a week for the next two months.

At some point, we did not have the time to look into the margins we made and the profits we got. But we knew we did earn a lot. After a while though, we hit a plateau we only made the same amount every month.

"You arranged for money?"The nurse at the reception asks.
"Yes," Sorya says.
"We can start the treatment, come over tomorrow."
"Okay"

We walk out of the hospital and walk towards a field where rice wine is sold.

"Have it"Sorya passes on the Jute covered Jug to me
"Finally we are going in the right direction," I say.
"I am not sure."
"About what?"
"About my treatment, I know I cannot live long anymore. We cannot waste this money on me."
"It is your life."
"I know, but why spend on a life which is destined to be short already? I do not believe the doctors in there."
"Then why did you rush for earning money"
"I wanted to earn as much as possible so that when I pass away, my family should be happy and rich."
"If you live, it is unparalleled to any riches you earn."
"Listen to me, Chan, I will take the treatment but for now let us postpone it, I have bigger plans and do not want to spoil them now by wasting this money,"Sorya says as he takes a huge gulp from a pitcher offered to him by the lady tending him the wine.
"You have something in your mind already,"I say.
"Yes, I do."
"What is it?"
"You know what is the most sought-after thing by people

here," He asks.

"Money"

"No, it is just a means to get something, guess further."

"Rice Wine,"I say as I lift my jug.

"Wrong"

"Land"

"No, everyone can afford to have it with money."

"Okay I give up,"

Sorya continues to drink and smiles at me.

"What is it?"

"You need to follow me"

"Why are you bragging too much, just tell me what it is"

"Medicine"

"What?"

"Yes people are crazy about it, they go to any extent to cure themselves with medicine,"

"I do not think that is true. You are a living example."

"I am not talking about those useless pills the doctor gives us, traditional medicine, from the wild,"

"You think that is useful?"

"We do not know, but it will help me to raise a lot of money,"

"You are going crazy these days."

"You must look at the money people spend on this stuff, and you would never call me crazy."

The next day we go to meet a man Sunse.

"Do you have your gear?" He asks.

"No, we do not need it,"Sorya says.

Sunse smiles sarcastically at us.

"Take this," He says.

"What is this for?"Sorya asks.

"A poisoned knife, do not use it on the animal unless needed to save your life"

"Okay,"Sorya says.

"How much for a crocodile?"

"Forget about it, with the way you are equipped, I doubt if you can get a monkey without being attacked."

"We have our weapons in the forest."

"So do your foolishness," Sunse says softly, as he subtly moves his bent head in disapproval on his angular spine.

We walk into the bushes leading to the forest trail created by the human path. The trail ends abruptly with dense trees hovering all over us. At this point, the sound of birds and rustling leaves is more dominant. No human voices, though the hurling of the wind through the grooves of the leaves is making sounds like a human whisper. Sorya walks towards a tree and cuts off a few branches with his axe hidden in his cloak. He drops some bananas and meat near the branches. He removes a knife from the bag and pours a slimy liquid poison on a knife retrieved from a tiny glass bottle with an air-tight lid, which he struggled to open. We climb up the tree and wait for an animal encounter. It was 6 30 PM and the light is slowly starting to fade.

"Shall we leave, it is getting dark gradually?"I say.

"You hear that?"

"What"

"Sound of the tiger"

"What?"

"You will catch a tiger?"

"Shh, Just stay silent, the real hunt is going to begin in a while"

After a few minutes, it is completely dark and mosquitoes started preying on us.

"Sorya, I think it is of no use"

"Stay silent."

"Think about it,"
"I am not going home without a hunt, today."

We hear sounds beneath us, the branches are dwindling haphazardly. An animal is below.

"Sorya," I say.
"Yes"
"Check out beneath"
"What happened"
"There is some animal."
"Claws Looks like a bear," He says.
"What will you do with it?"
"We will see, let us take it for now."

Sorya jumps to the lower branches and makes a jump aiming the stick with the knife tied to its end going straight into the neck. After a few moments, I cautiously get down the tree.

"Not a bear," I say.
"I know,"Sorya says.
"It is a baboon,"
"I don't think there will be any market for this grown monkey."
"What shall we do?"
"Let us give it another try."
"But do you have another knife?"
"I have a knife but it is not poisoned."
"And you came to kill a tiger."

Sorya slays the animal again with another strike, a lot of shrieking and groaning happens and the voice fades into the woods as it breathes its last.

"Come down,"Sorya says.
It was not as easy as we climbed up, nor there is a drive to kill something to jump audaciously.

We walk a few meters ahead.

"Sun bear"

"It is worthy."

"Let's find out."

We dump the bear into a jute bag which is short of size. The legs of the bear are partially outside, which we covered with branches of trees.

After walking for an hour, we reach the city trade market.

"We have a catch,"Sorya says to the man.

"Come inside,"He says as he leads inside his trade exhibits in the mud hut.

"Show me."

"Sun Bear"

"Dead," He asks.

"Probably"

"Throw it away, it is as good as your nails,"

"I thought it was in demand."

"Do your homework. It is worth only while alive not when dead."

Disappointed we leave the place and burnt the bear in an open field. A life wasted for nothing.

After five months we are adept at trafficking pangolins for their scales. Money made is at par when compared to what we are earning earlier by selling small stuff yet this is an incredible transformation. We killed 50 pangolins in a month at our peak.

We trained wild dogs referred to as "Dhole" to help retrieve and assist in killing small prey. We managed to pull off a tiger but it did escape and died solitarily, its body never to be found. Tiger fur has great demand.

Our reputation has doubled in the trading community. We opened a shop for ourselves in the city. Rhino horns are most sought after by white people from abroad. By hiring new hunters and training our dogs we managed to kill tigers. Almost every part of the tiger is sold high. Even the whiskers of a tiger are sold for money. Our customers are everywhere from India, China, America and the Middle East.

Sorya had his occasional fits, but he has recovered well. He is getting the best treatment available and travelled to China more than once to cure his illness.

It has been three years, and I did not go to the village. I brought my Oxen to the village and have been taken care of. My hut is still there. After a long time, I wanted to see my hut, the well and Champa. I also had some scores to settle.

I walk to my hut and see it covered in dead leaves and dust. A few of my workers have come along with me, they helped to clean it. I rented it out to a local farmer who approached me through one of my hunting men.

My men cycle towards Champa's place and I look at the house, but Yiey is not there. I signal the men to move forward. I am at the place where I was kicked and beaten black and blue. I walk towards the hut and knock on the door.

A middle-aged man in his fifties or maybe the forties opens the door. It takes a while for me to recognize him. He was one of them who attacked me. I extend a handshake to him. I grab his hand swing it towards his feet and with a sharpened knife I cut his little finger off. He screams so loud that his gang comes outside rushing to attack me. I whistle at my hunter's team and they yield their poisoned knives gashing each one of them randomly. After a moment they realize that the knives are poisoned, and they rush towards Yiey's house. I chase them as they run with their clothes drenched in blood wetting the ground with maroon patches.

I walk over to the home and now Yiey is directly staring at me.

"Go away, you evil man, I am not going to let you meet Champa,"She says to me.

"I am sorry Yiey. I do not need your permission, please take care of your men. I thank you for making me realize what I am worth by sending these men to me."

I walk away from the place, grab my cycle and follow towards my hut with my team trailing behind.

Yiey dies while sleeping the next day. Uninvited I attend the funeral to meet Champa.

I walk towards Champa whose face is swollen with grief.

"She is everything to me," She says

"I know,"I say as I hug her.

In a moment she steps back, maybe she realized how much I have changed. I am wearing a watch with a silver bracelet, tailored clothes, gold chains and rings. I am also using perfume.

"You cannot be here Champa. I have earned well, come with me, I love you."

"I cannot leave this place,"Champa says.

"Even I thought so until I left."

"Please leave, this is not the right moment."

"This is the moment I say."

Watching me and Champa debate, a few men steps ahead towards me. I stare at them and they leave. They are very well aware now of what I can do by now.

The next day I leave the village and walk towards the boat to go to the city. All our cycles are loaded onto separate boats. Sorya is in the city to manage the trade while I was in the village. The boats are set into motion and as we move a few yards away I hear a voice. It is Champa shouting at me.

"Chann" she screams.

It has been five years since I heard that scream and we never went back to the village. I married Champa with all pomp and show in the city. Champa is still not aware of the business I do completely. I have earned quite well in these years more than I could do whole my life in the village. The blood shed by the animals, the hunt, the brawls and the fight towards dominance in the trade all led to this day, I recollect this while I am sipping my coffee standing on the patio looking at Champa and the servants working in the garden. Sorya and me together we hunted many tigers, we have a team. We set traps known to study their migration patterns and make the kill. Sorya got himself almost killed after being remorseful for drawing his knife into the belly of a pregnant tiger, he did not strike further. The tiger, half alive, pounced back on him and snatched his left arm. We could not release the tiger from him for thirty minutes. Sorya lost his left arm. His survival was not easy, it was a trauma for all of us. We understood one thing that day. You hunt or back off, if struck in thought you can get killed. Sorya never came to the fields to hunt after that. He is doing small business and sometimes joins me in striking a bargain or making a deal. After losing his arm, Sorya had many ailments and health issues but with money and doctors at his disbursal, we can keep him alive. Kala is now relieved that her husband is breathing.

At 10 30 PM it was raining heavily, we gathered around the dining table with the dinner served and ready. Rice dumplings, Chicken wings and beef steak were served. The room is lit with candles, flames popping up and down seen by the shadows on the wall. Some days we also share the table with our helpers. The idea of making money is in my mind but the distinction in lifestyle is still strange to me. I think each of these helpers would have a hut like me in their village at which they would have lived. There was a huge thunder followed by a rumble.

"You hear that," Champa says to me.

"Yes"

"It reminds me of the horridness of the bombings"

"Forget it"

"No one in the city can"

"I know, stay happy that now it is better."

"I feel like a calmness before the storm."

"The Americans got what they wanted, there is no reason for them to storm, pass me the steak," I say.

"If not for the bombings my hearing would have been better."

"I spoke to the doctor. Your hearing can naturally restore, or we may go for a minor device to enhance the reception."

"I don't want any devices hanging on my ear, please bear with me and manage,"

We finish the dinner along with our helpers who eat along with us shyly.

"Where is your son? He joins us for dinner usually," I ask our helper lady Mao.

"I am sorry for that Sir. He is sick and could not come."

"You left him at home?"

"Yes, I had to isolate him. I am worried if contagious. I came for the duties of the house, not to worry I am not staying with him for now."

"Alright, take him to the hospital and do not delay,"Champa says.

"Mao, you can leave after dinner and take leave for a few days, help him recover, your expenses will be taken care of, Meet me later"

"Thanks, Sir," Mao says.
We finish the dinner by talking about happenings in the city and random hearsay news from helpers.

A shark has swallowed and bit me until my waist. I am unable to move, numb in my legs. I gather all the energy in my body and kick hard, I fell on the floor and hurt my back. I am out of the dream. Champa is tucked into the bed, wrapped in a quilt.

"What happened ?" she utters to me with eyes closed
"Nothing"

I take the stairs and walk to the entrance of the house. Smoke is rising from somewhere, and the smell is strong. I usher to open the door, but it is locked from the outside. I was unable to breathe. I could hear Champa coughing. The furniture inside the house is lit by fire. Curtains are blazing yellow.

I pick a wooden chair and throw it on the glass of the window door. A spider web form crack in the glass but it is not fully open. One more hit and the glass falls off to the ground. In a couple of minutes, I break the glass of 4 more windows. The smoke is pungent and strong, and I could see Champa's nose bleed. With one more attempt, I break all the small glass cone residue on the window. Champa fetches her boots and jumps out of the door. I manage to get out in my leather sandals. We rush onto the lawn and fall on the ground facing the night sky gasping for air. As we get into our senses, I pick a hose pipe and direct the jet of water inside the house towards the curtains. Soon passersby and our workers arrive, they take the pipe from my hand and draw water from a nearby well and seize the fire shortly. We thank them.

"Be careful, the Khmer Gang is gaining momentum. They are targeting the Vietnamese, all educated middle class and the rich" Nodding her head incessantly due to a disorder could be, she advises Champa.

We sleep on the grass for the next couple of hours as everyone leaves.

"I am worried," Champa says.

"Do not" That was just a random fire.

"No, it was planned, how did they light it from inside."

"We have to investigate. It could be the candles."

"The candles were all off when I went to bed."

"Do not take it too seriously."

"You heard what the lady said."

"Yes"

"What do we do about it?"

"We do what the Prince did."

"Flee the city?"

"Yes"

"Where do we go?

"Your country"

"How? Is it true?

"Yes, I is it all arranged."

"But what do we do with our money and property here?"

"I will sort it out later."

"I have to tell you something."

"What is it?"

"Nothing.We'll tell you later, not on this day."

The next morning I summon our workers and ask each of them what time they left the house. No matter how much I inquire I find no answer on what caused the fire.

Lady Mao starts crying.

"What is it?"I ask.

"I am sorry, I failed as a mother."

"What happened, is your son alright."

"He is no longer my son."

"What is it Mao?" I ask, Champa stands beside me concerned and intrigued by the response.

"It was my son and his cadres who did it."

"What?"

"Yes, it is he who did it."

"I overheard him talking to his group near a lane beside my house while I was reaching home, they are checking on everyone in the neighbourhood and reporting to the leaders of the rouge who later give them instructions to create panic, he hardly came home for weeks, they are staying away isolated from here. I pretended that I knew nothing, but I could not hide the fact of what he had done to you."

"So you knew he would attack us"

"No No, I knew after they did it, yesterday night."

"Should I talk to him?"

"I do not know Sir. He is no longer the same person I knew before, he calls me by my name which he never did earlier, and he does not show any emotion on his face. All I know is they doing something heinous."

"Alright, bring him here. I will talk to him some time."

"Thanks, Sir, I will, I can work here further?"

"Yes, this is a small issue. We can settle it, do not fear, he needs some counselling."

"I am kind of relieved now," Champa says as the workers disburse.

I smile at her.

"What is it,"

"I think we have a problem," I say.

"Why, how can you be so sure?"

"I had a bad dream," I say,

"I told you that I have to tell you something but you did not ask for it."

"Yes what is it?

"It will lighten up your day."

"You have to tell me now."

"Close your eyes," Champa says as she grabs both my hands and places them on her stomach.

"What?"I look at her partly figuring out what it could be.

"Yes," She says indicating it to be true.

"Is it true?"

"Yes, you are going to be a father."

I lift Champa and turn her around in circles, jumping for joy.

I go to the city and try to enquire about the Khmer Rouge. I visit Sorya later in the day.

"I told you not to get that mansion," Sorya says.

"Why?"

"You are causing trouble for yourself by showing your wealth."

"It is not to show Sorya. I wanted Champa to be happy."

"What do you do now,"

"I must go to India"

"India? Why?"

"I will settle there and come here for business."

"You know that the British have colonized India and would not let you stay in the mansion either."

"I do not know, maybe once the situation improves we can come back."

"I have some friends in India; I will move the cash as commodities not to worry, for the rest it would take some time."

"Weeks?"

"Two months"

"Okay"

"Join us for dinner tomorrow along with Kala"

"Any occasion?"
"I am going to be a father."
"Wonderful, that is great news, we will be there"

The roads are wet with rain. Trees seem tired, withered by the rain and wind. The skies are dark with clouds. It is just six in the evening but there is no light in the sky except for the faint hint of dull light seeping between the clouds. I walk along the road to my home and could hear the chatter of the frogs croaking. As I enter, there is no one on the lawn. The servants would not have come owing to the rain. I see the doors wide open. There is no one in the hall. The lights are lit, and lunch is on the table served on the plate half eaten.

"Champa! Champa!"I shout but no response.
I walk to the street and see no trace of her. Two teens upon seeing me from a distance start to run. I run after them chasing for two lanes in wet and mud. I slipped at once but not to miss them I keep my sight on them. They finally stop at an armed jeep. I walk slowly towards them checking if they have a gun ready to fire.

"Get in" Someone has pointed a rifle at my back.

I walk towards the jeep and see AK47 rifles with the two teens. I get into the jeep in the rear with one adult, and two teens sitting in front of me with their guns pointed at me.

"Keys," he asks.
"What keys?"I say.
"Your mansion"
"It is unlocked."
"Where is my wife?"I ask him, to whom he does not answer.
"Where is she? You need money I can give you, how much you want, and we will leave the city, take me to her," I say.
"Quiet," he says.

After an hour's drive, they take me to a village and with the mud and rain, one of the wheels got stuck in a thick puddle. Even after pushing the jeep, they could not get it out. I get down for a moment.

"I can help you," I say.

"Push"

I pretend that I am pushing and grab one of the rifles from the teen, point towards them and run backwards. After some distance, I turn in the direction I am heading and began to run. A thought struck my mind what if they are taking me to where they captured Champa? I stood still unable to decide if I should run or go back. Meanwhile, I could hear a jeep coming in my direction which halted abruptly after seeing me.

"Take me to my wife," I say with a rifle in my hand.

"What is her name?"They ask.

"Champa," I say.

"Okay get in we know her, will take you," They say, everyone is staring at me, my dress dirtied by the mud and my hair wet in the rain.

I get into the jeep with the rifle on my lap. They stop near the jeep I came in earlier which got stuck in the mud. The driver gets down and walks towards him. I bend over trying to hide from them, I draw the sheet at the door used for protection from the rain. Our driver hooks up the jeep and pulls their jeep out of the mud. We drive for thirty minutes with the jeep trailing us, my heart is beating like a galloping horse. After a while, I could see the trailing jeep take a turn in another direction. I feel relieved for now yet not sure where Champa is.

"Let us have some Tea," the driver says to all of us.

I got down at the stall and sit on a rock thinking if Champa was still in the house and I did not search properly, many thoughts run my mind. Am I stuck in this situation by myself? Dark thoughts seem to cloud my mind, yet I try to steer away from them. In a single hard breath from the shock of someone striking the back of my head very hard with a rifle, I collapse to the ground. I could faintly see the horizon as I am picked up by them and dumped into the rear of the jeep in between the seatings. With my head facing the trail, I could also see the jeep in which I was picked earlier following us.

I wake up in a closed brick room with one dim halogen bulb lit by my side. The floor is wet and stinking. As I touch my mouth, I could feel something slimy and sticky. I check my hand after touching my chin. I could feel it is my blood and vomit. My jaw is aching, they had hit me. I do not have my shirt on and in my pants only. My watch is not on my wrist. There is a chair in the room far away. I am chained on one of my legs. I gradually fade out into unconsciousness. I am in a deep abyss, a vacuum in which life transforms into death. I could feel the pain being inflicted upon me now and then. Electric shocks are inflicted on me now and then which is preventing me from dying by the guards. With a horrific stream of current leaving me I wake consciously. I passed stools in my pants, and the stench is unbearable. The teens dressed in grey uniforms with red scarves around their necks are taking turns to visit me and laugh at my state. There is a gap in the mud bricks. I limped towards it unable to walk. From the gap in the bricks, I could see the sky so dark, it is late at night. There is a bulb hanging onto a tree. A child was in the hands of one of the soldiers while he was talking to the other. It was probably more than a day since I have been here or maybe it was the day I came here, I forgot why I came here. The shocks made my mind delusional. Why did I come here? Why am I being prisoned here? Suddenly I hear loud shrieks of a baby crying in agony. I look into the gap in the bricks. The baby is lying beside the tree, bleeding. The Khmer gang member picked up the child again and bashed it into the tree again with impact to the head, there were loud shrieks of the baby crying desperately. The child would be no more than a year. With one more hit to the tree, the baby calms to death and a woman is heard screaming to the top of her voice in pain and desperation, it could be her mother. As if nothing has happened the cadres pick up the baby and dump it into a stash bin.

I am kicked to my senses by the crying mother who reminds me of Champa.

"Champa! Champa!"I shout aloud.

A group of Khmer men enter and kick me in my stomach and bang my head against the brick wall. Strangely I am ceasing to fall unconscious after what I have just seen. The dead baby is killing my inability to escape and save her. I want to know where is my wife. I cannot imagine her imprisoned here. I could hear screams of men shouting to the highest pitch. The next moment I woke up is I dying of thirst. The stench is heavy, I am feeling weak in every inch of my body, it has been days since I ate. I think this is the place where people think death is better than life. I looked at the lizard on the wall. Hunger is killing me to the point I felt I had to eat it to stay alive. I picked it up by my hand bit the tail with my mouth and threw it on the ground. I chewed it and burst into tears. I could not swallow it and vomited it to the floor. I am crying uncontrollably, reminded me of my mother when she had gone through torture while trying to protect me from stones pelting at her. My mother is not here to shield me. I miss the comfort in her lap. Where is Champa? The thought that if Campa is caught by these rouges is haunting me every minute. For the next few hours, I fall asleep which I hope can lead to death.

The Khmer guards kick me into consciousness and drag me into another room which is cleaner but stinking with human faces and blood. There is a cot and a chair to which electric wires are fastened. The Khmer guards picked me up and strapped me to the chair.

CHAPTER NINE

2016 Singapore

Narrator: Priya

It is a bright sunny morning. I woke up to the sunshine from the horizon beaming onto the glass in my bedroom. What a nice day. I switch into my running tracks and sweatshirt and go for a run along a road winding through the row of houses and villas. Donny my lab is out with me running along. He pulls heavily on the leash initially but after a few meters, he slows down to my pace gradually. It was raining heavily at night, so the ground is still wet and the fragrance of the flowers is being felt. I updated my playlist yesterday which is helping me to run longer than usual but my dog already started panting. I slow down to a jogging pace. My phone is now ringing inside the armband. I answer it on my earphone call button.

"Hello," I say.

"Hi Priya"

"Tevy?"

"Yes it's me."

"How are you?"

"I am good."

"How about you?"

"I am fine, came out for a jog with my dog."

"Cool"
"I had everything sorted out, motion sensors in place, hope this should give us some insight."
"This is the only hope I have Priya."
"Don't worry, we will catch hold of him."
"It is still not conclusive."
"I know, I mean if he is the one"
"My gut says he did it, yet I am still confused,"
"I would suggest you give some time, the truth will reveal for itself."
"Okay"
"When will you be here?"
"In a week,"
"He agreed?"
"Not yet, I still need to make a few moves and we will be there."
"Alright then"
"Go ahead with your jog, we can talk later"
"How is your mother doing?
"She is fine, dealing with helpers who come on and off leaving her with the errands."
"You should change her helper."
"Yes, I need to find some time for that, occupied with dealing with him."
"I get it."
"Cya"
"C you, bye"

I lost my momentum, and Donny is comfortably sitting staring at me.

"Alright, let's go around a few more blocks and then we fetch groceries and go home," I say to Donny

He wags his tail and follows me. He loves going around shops and sniffing around the wet market as they wouldn't let him in for obvious reasons.

We reach home. I mince the chicken and drop it into the pressure cooker for it to boil along with some veggies and brown rice. While I am cooking, I notice that the kitchen does not have a CC camera, looks like they missed it.

"Hello"

"Hi Madam"

"You missed the camera in the Kitchen."

"You need one in the kitchen as well?"

"I told you not to miss any portion of the house."

"Alright Mam we will be there by Sunday"

"No, it will be too long, I need to test them, please make it early."

"Okay Mam will try tomorrow"

I miss Sophea. Tevy is very different from her sister. At this point, I have no clue if I go in the right direction by following Tevy. We had to do this to find the truth about what happened to Sophea.

I still remember Sophea's funeral, her mom did not shed a tear. Yet her brown eyes were so dark and deep, she would have seen that darkness that loomed over her daughter. She did not utter a word could be since everyone around her are too shallow in their thoughts for her. What was running through her mind was more than just losing her daughter. She knew Tevy was hiding the reason for her sisters' death, and she did ask about it. Tevy and her mother did not speak much during the entire funeral, but they exchanged conversation with mere eyes. Something was running deep in the family. It was so silent at the grave that we could hear the flutter of the butterflies and the buzzing of the bees on the flowers.

After some time, four black range rovers stormed through the entrance and came right towards the cemetery.

Parking was not allowed inside. The gatekeeper came inside to tell them to vacate, he was tipped with a five hundred dollar bill by a man dressed in all white and a political party flag posted on the bonnet of his vehicle. In a moment, the silence was gone. Party men were talking in loud voices among themselves and on their phones. One of the men walked towards Tevy's mother with folded hands.

"Namaste"

"I am sorry for your loss."

Tevy's mother did not utter a word.

"I will find."

"No need for all that,"Tevy's mom says interrupting his speech. My daughter will take care.

"Okay, it was never safe to be alone, take my protection, all this should not have happened."

"Come with me" Tevy gently pulls her mom aside breaking their conversation.

As they walk silently away from him,

"Why did he come here?"Tevy asks.

"You need to find out."

"What protection is he talking about? He is after us for money. You know that.

"You need to find who killed your sister."

"No one killed her mother. It was an accident,"Tevy says.

"You know the truth if not you will, you do not have to console me."

"Sorry Aunt,"I say as I just realized that I barged into their private moment, they remain silent looking at me, while Aunt holds my hand and walks me further to the burial place.

"I saw her yesterday in my dream, she should not have passed away so soon, whoever did this will have to suffer,"Aunt says.

I nod in agreement at her not knowing what to say.

We had all cameras installed and everything ready. I felt it was my responsibility to find the truth.

"Do we really need to do this?"Tevy asks me.

"We have come so far Tevy, there is no point in giving up now."

"How close are you to getting the truth"

"I do not know, sometimes I feel he is the one and sometimes that he is not."

"You got any clue."

"Until now, I haven't heard him say a single word about Sophea, if he really did it, he is very criminal, as he lacks guilt of any sort. He is thinking about something sometimes but never saying anything to me."

That was our last conversation after Tevy came to Singapore. She is supposed to call me today instead I got a message from her.

"Come to General Hospital at 8 PM. I am hit by a bike... and you know nothing about this..meet me privately. delete this message."

I am confused, is she really hit by a bike or is she faking it? Whatever it is, I will go.

I checked about Tevy at the reception, luckily it was quite busy so I did not have to give my details. I sneaked towards the open door opposite her room. There was a chair beside the bed and both are empty. I could see Arka and Tevy in the room. Arka was walking back and forth and he glanced at Tevy's face in deep thought. I was waiting for him to leave. Arka sat on the chair beside Tevy and was never leaving. I preposterously walked into another room with an empty bed and sat on the chair. I dozed off for a while in the chair.

"Wake up, Wake up" Tevy had me startled by her sudden jerk on my shoulder.

"Tevy!! Are you fine? How are you?"

"I am good, we do not have much time, he will come back."

"Are you really hurt?"

"Yes I am, I am really hurt by the biker who hit me but not so much that I needed to be admitted here. I thought of using this as an opportunity to know more about Arka"

"Careful Tevy"

"I know."

"Where is he?"

"He would have gone for a smoke."

"Alright"

"I called earlier so that you do not panic,"

"I think he will be back shortly."

"Should I leave?

"No, talk to him when he is here and let me know what you feel about him."

"I am not so good at that."

"No you do not need to be friendly with him, keep a serious tone and stay on the point, asses his thoughts if you can."

"Okay but what if he asks me how I knew you were here,"

"Just tell him that someone answered my phone and told you that I am here, probably the nurse, do not worry he does not fret much about such details, which sometimes makes me feel in case if he is not really guilty."

"Do not jump to conclusions."

"Ya I know Priya. It is just a feeling."

"Alright sit back and relax, have this juice and the burger."

"Grab me those cookies, I will skip the burger," Tevy says as she sips on the orange juice.

CHAPTER TEN

2016 Singapore

Narrator: Arka

It has been three days since I came back to Malaysia. Priya insisted I traveled back after waiting for a week. Tevy hasn't gained consciousness yet. I will be going to Singapore again in two days to check on Tevy's condition. I picked up my Oscar fish from the pet store where I handed them over. I had a bad experience with the automated feeder in the past, so I generally give them for petting during my travels. I got a call on my phone.

"Hi"

"Hello"

"It's me."

"Tevy? How are you, I just came today" I say.

"I know, Priya told me."

"I will start now."

"No, that's alright, I will be there soon, you can stay there."

"How are you feeling now?"

"I feel much better."

I wake up with a sudden jerk to see my phone ring.

"Hi"

"Hello"

"It's me."

"Tevy?"I say startled knowing that I was dreaming, and Tevy called.
"You went today is it, Priya told me."
"Yes"
"You stay there, I will be fine in a few days, will come back."
"Okay"

I disconnect the phone.

I pour the sizzling water from my kettle into Nissin cup noodles. The aroma gives a feeling of the crab nibbles inside. I walk towards the window and sit there, placing my cup on the wall of the balcony. My phone is ringing. I ignore it and continue to stare at the blue sky and the swirling cars and bikes around the junction of the road.

What is this feeling over here, I feel like I am inside a balloon filled with hot air. I only tend to believe that the air is breathable but for every passing moment. I am consuming the oxygen and choking myself.

The phone rings again, and it is Priya saying the same as before. I walk towards the kitchen and notice my phone being charged. Now I walk back to where I attended the call earlier only to notice that my phone is no longer there. Did it learn to walk? Never mind I stopped bothering about such events anymore.

I pick up my phone and go down my flat towards the basement and on the road. I dial in Priya's number.

"Hi Priya"
"Hi Arka"
"How is she?
"She gained consciousness for a brief moment. Doctors are positive."
"That is great, thank you"
"That's it? How are you?
"M good, called to check up on her"

"Fine then, Cya"
"Priya!"
"Yes, tell me,"
"Did you call me earlier?
"I tried reaching you once when you just left but I could not reach you. I tried calling you today but I think you are out of the coverage area as it says."
"Okay, ya I went elsewhere"
"That's Alright, take care, she will be fine soon as we hope."

I trace back to my apartment and sit on the balcony viewing the sparrow dropping twigs on the window pane. The nesting of a bird is so strange before it settles for laying eggs. Some of them lose their nest with time, yet they make a new place their home bonding with them like the former. Nila seems to be nesting wherever I am or it would be my nesting of her free will and preventing her to escape. How can I explain it to her? She is suffering, and I am caught up in the abyss of darkness surrounding her soul which is not yet freed.

I see a motorcycle parked at the beginning of the street, it has been there for a while. I try to recollect seeing the guy standing beside it.No clue of knowing yet, but I have seen him very recently. He wore a blue half-sleeved shirt and white flying birds print all over it.

I walk inside to fetch my Marlboro pack which I bought for Tevy. I place the cigarette in my mouth and recollect that I need a lighter. I walk towards my closet open a drawer and pick up my zippo. I flick the wheel which oozes sparkles out of the top lid but no flame. I stand on my toes to pick a bottle of refill for my lighter and spray it into the canister. After a few flicks, the flame is loud and bright, I lit the cigarette and walk to my balcony. As I stare at the road two guys on a rat bike probably a 300cc Duke watched me and started muttering among them suspiciously. If they are keeping a watch on me and pretending not to, they would be very bad at acting. Why would they anyway? I notice that my cigarette is not a Marlboro, but I have placed menthol in this pack for some reason not sure. This is not bad either especially on a sunny day. I sit on the chair. Why did I get the same call again with the same message? Is it Nila doing this? it has been a while since I thought about Nila. I have to tell Tevy about my hallucinations someday. The kid with the balloon I saw on this street why does he appear always with the balloon? I do not know. But when he does, I only see him. I exist at that moment as that kid holding the balloon trying to save it from the boys who want to cease it. The boy is now standing on the street. The lad on the Duke is sticking his phone out to take a picture of me while momentarily glancing away. But why? Runs in the mind of the boy. After a couple of more clicks, they go away. This routine goes on for a few days at a point I considered them to be part of my life and at some other point, I thought they were genuinely engaged in their own business and had nothing to do with me.

Today is not another day, sometimes I accept life the way it is. Never try to fix it. It happened with Nila, I knew there is a catastrophe ahead but I never focused on making things right. I am having my shower. The guys are there beside the boy waiting for me. Yesterday they followed me after having a few drinks at Tapas. There are three men today not two. The boy with the balloon lets it float. I am holding the showerhead in my hand. I close my eyes and meditate on the sound of the water sizzling from the nozzles of the head. The sound of water is very much subjective to the way it is released. As frightening as the sound of a waterfall could be, the sound of the waves of the sea can soothe your mind. Now, this water is only making me meditate deeply on each droplet piercing through the air and hitting me. I open my eyes holding the balloon in my hand. The third guy is facing away from me while the other two I have known for a few days. The silhouette of the third one is familiar. I run into the streets holding the balloon and as I do the darkness of the cumulonimbus cloud hovers over me growing closer to the ground every second and plunging me forward into the converging horizon.

"Stop there," I say as I hold the shirt of a third one

With that, the face-tanned Malay, a Chinese with beads on his arm, and neck, a fair-looking local with punk hair, and a tattoo on his face across the temple and neck started their bikes, a 300cc Duke and a Kawasaki z900. I can recognize the punk guy. He tried to speed away when I spotted him at the hospital. They are a mile ahead when I go towards my Burgman. Luckily I placed a spare of my BMW G1000 keys in the storage of my scooter. I take the keys and rush towards them with my rear tire making a hot black patch of rubber burnt while rolling on the ground. The green pine leaves rustle to the slight wind, while the three bike engines are whirring along the lane below heading towards an end not yet reached. The Kawasaki managed to throttle so that it is much further from me while the Duke is an easy catch. I have to make the decision, hold which one. The kid on the duke is probably involved for money, and he may not be having full information but if I could catch him, I can uncover at least the details of his partner. I race ahead of the Duke and skid my rear tire grabbing the clutch and pressing on the foot pedal. My rear tire was just inches short of stopping his front wheel. He tries to cut through the edge and narrowly runs away. I accelerate towards him and follow. I disengage the traction control on my bike. With only a pair of gloves in my tank bag and a power bank, I recently purchased there is nothing else in it. This time I do not overtake him even if I could. I maintained a steady speed so that I could go in parallel to his bike. I pick the power bank from my tank bag and aim for his head while I also bump my front wheel into his rear probably if he had a helmet could have saved the impact and managed to move away. With two launches at once, he loses control of the bike and drifts onto the side road gradually flapping like a butterfly and falling onto the tarmac. His fingers were visibly bruised. I walk toward him. He would be probably in his twenties.

"What is your problem?" he asks me.

"Well I should be asking that," I say.

At 10:30 PM I pack my things to go to Singapore. I take a rental car as my bike needs some servicing, though it had not suffered much damage from the impact. I have to see Tevy and talk to her. My mind is clouded with thoughts unable to understand what is going on. Why did she have to do this, should I still trust her? Why do I still feel like I care for her? Did she ever love me? What is her motto? She could not have faked an accident I saw her taking the hit. Why does she have to deploy men to follow me? I did not get all the answers I need. Every answer is leading to another question. There is no way she could have known about Nila, did she? Probably I should have told her. I do not know but Nila is not alive. It does not make any difference.

With many thoughts running through my mind, I covered the distance from the hall to the patio.

"Hello Sir"
"Hi"
"ID please"
"Yup," I hand over as he looks at my number plate and makes an entry at Priya's condo.

I head towards the flat and wait a minute before ringing the bell.

Am I doing it right? This is an uninformed visit. Priya might feel embarrassed. But I cannot tell her all that happened over the phone, not sure even if Priya is involved. I look at the shoe rack and see knives and a Katana on it. Who would have placed it? I walk towards the door and look into the peephole nothing clear or interesting. I could hear low rumbling sounds. I bang on the door calling for Priya. I also rang the bell. No use. The door could be locked from the inside. Not sure. I wait for five minutes and walk downwards to the entrance security of the condo.

"Is the lady of flat 304 away," I ask the security.
"No Sir"
"Who was her last visitor?"
"Sorry Sir but why are you asking?"
"I got no response at the door so a bit worried."
"A lady named Tevy visited today morning Sir and none after that"
"Tevy, strange"
"How did she come?"
"She came in a taxi, Sir."
"Did she leave already?
"We only track the entry, Sir."
"Alright, I will check again if they open the door."

I reach their flat and knock on the door again but no response. They would have left as security may not have noticed the exit.

I walk towards the lift and enter it, as the doors are about to close, I notice someone outside. I exit on the next floor down and rush towards the stairs and walk towards the entrance. There are no knives or katana present earlier. I bang on the door this time I hear a little voice shriek. Something is not right. I use the duplicate key that I got from Tevy earlier and forgot to hand it over. I use it to unlock the door, with slight hesitation, I enter the hall feeling that I may have barged into someone's privacy. To my shock, two guys are sitting on the sofa watching TV and startled by my entry.

"Who are you?" they ask.

"I am Priya's friend, who are you ?"

"We are her cousins."

"I came for Priya,"

"She went on vacation last month and did not come yet"

"Alright," I say as I figure out something fishy.

"Can I use the washroom?" I say.

"Why not" They stare at each other and say

"There is some issue with the sink flush though needs some plumbing work," they say after some gap.

"I guess there are three washrooms in here."

"Ya, you can use"

As they nod their heads in confusion leading different ways for me.

I rush inside without waiting for another silly reason from them. By now I know there is something wrong.

I sit in the loo for five minutes thinking about the situation, I could see duct tape and a pair of scissors placed near the basin. There are also face masks thrown beside.

I open the door slightly to notice that both of them are standing opposite the door blockading the view to the bedroom on the left.

"What," they ask.

"Nothing," I say as I fully open the door and exit.

One of them a tall grey-haired and crested face with blotches on his forehead noticed the tape and masks. He knew that I was having my suspicions.

"We have to go for lunch" shall we leave they say to me.

"Oh sorry for bothering you and wasting your time, I am done, we can leave," I say.

"I have forgotten my Zippo here on my last visit, I say lying to them walking towards the bedroom rapidly."

"Hello mister, now leave us, have entertained you too much, not sure even if you know Priya," they say as they pounce upon me.

I push them back and rush into the rooms to notice Tevy and Priya both seated at two corners with their mouth taped and hands tied.

I pick up all my energy and give a hard blow to the silver-haired man on his face. I slap the other. They pull out their knives and try to slash me in my neck. I move back, kicking my foot into his groin. In pain, he falls back. The dark-haired one shorter than the other gets his katana from the hall. I pick the white Ikea light stand longer than Katana and hurl it towards his face. The bulb and glass case enclosing it fell on his leg. As he moves back I kick on his wrist. The katana dropped to the floor, poor choice of weapon in an enclosed space. I rush forward standing on the katana while also hurling two more kicks at the groin each. I pick up the dropped knife from the silver hair guy and threaten them. I untie the knots of Tevy keeping the knife facing them. Tevy removes the knot of Priya. Tevy rushes to her mobile to call the police as she begins to dial the number, the short guy snatches it from her hand

and runs towards the door dropping it on the floor and breaking the screen with the sole of his boot. All of them rush towards the door now and escape. As I try to follow them, Tevy holds my hand stopping me.

"No don't"

"Why?"

"I get it, is this another of your planned drama over me?"

"Excuse me."

"Forget it."

"Are you fine?"I ask.

She turns her arm, which is profusely bleeding and dripping blood onto the floor.

I look at Priya as she goes to fetch the first aid, Kit.

"Loan shark?"

"What!!" Priya says with an irritated expression on her face.

"I know you must have been angry with me,"Tevy says.

"I don't know what I am, but I can say, I cannot trust you anymore."

"I understand but let me explain to you," Tevy says.

"You say that all this is not about me or something which I will be easily made a fool of and trust you again? Never mind, forget it, you are wounded, take care, I do not have anything to talk to or hear to."

"Arka please listen," Priya says as she glances at Tevy and me rapidly.

I walk towards the balcony attached to the kitchen and stand there. I pick my Marlboro and lit a cigarette.

Meanwhile, I could sense that Tevy and Priya are just behind me in the kitchen.

"Coffee," Priya asks me.

"No... errr .. Okay," I say as I feel I am pushing a bit more in her house whatever differences I cannot vent out in her house.

Priya places the milk to boil, and she goes to fetch the first aid kit. I glance at Tevy concerned but not uttering a word.

Tevy avoids a direct look at me. We are in an awkward situation as we want to avoid a direct conversation. Those few minutes felt very long in silence.

After a few minutes of more silence and my cigarette burned off, I threw it into the bin after wiping the last few flames with the iron hand rest. Tevy was startled as I rushed toward her in an embracing move. I held her by her shoulders and moved her to switch off the stove on which the boiling milk was about to overflow. Realizing it, Tevy's heartbeat returned to normalcy.

Priya came back with a first aid kit and started applying some ointment on Tevy's wounds.

"May I know why we are not calling the police?"I ask.

Priya while holding the hand of Tevy applying ointment looks at her indicating for her to respond.

"I know who did it?" says Tevy.

I shrug in response.

"The person who sent those men is my uncle, brother of my mother. He was once my guardian but I never knew he was after our wealth and money."Tevy says.

"Okay, where is he in Singapore? Should you not inform the police?"

"No he is in India. My mother is also residing in the same district, if I try anything, they are powerful people who can hurt my mom," She says.

"Why would he hurt his sister?"

"I used the same rationale for so long, but I am wrong, he killed my sister Sophea, your dead wife, now he is after me."

"What!! You are the sister of Sophea?"

"Yes, I was after you as I suspected you of the murder of my sister. I tried every possible way to know you and bring you to the court of law. But you are non-existent in the media or the internet. I could not get you. Yes, I had a coveted operation on knowing who you are. You had a bad reputation with the doctors by the way. Having no presence in social life is generally attributed to a bad one usually. Only after dating you, I could relate to how you are. But never you spoke about Sophea. Though I could see you are disturbed a lot. We made a file on you but never found anything. Very recently my Uncle confessed to my mother about the killing of my sister and didn't hesitate to kill me if I do not marry his son."

"So all the love you spoke is an act."

Tevy remains silent.

"I can explain," Priya says.

"Please,"I say.

"Tevy wanted to stop this investigation on you when she started to like you. It was me who did not want her to. I was not sure about you. Which is because I never know you as Tevy did."

"Can I leave?"I ask.

"Never stopped you,"Tevy says.

"Hold on, don't do that,"Priya says.

I walk out of the house and take the lift towards my vehicle in the parking lot. I lit another cigarette trying to recollect all that which has happened with Tevy. I am unable to comprehend which is a true moment and which was not.

Tevy comes over and is standing right in front of me.

"You have anything else to ask me,"Tevy asks.

"Yes"

"What?"

"Did you ever love me?"

"I did Arka. I loved you always, somehow deep within me I always trusted you. It was my responsibility as a sister to find the truth. I always hoped it was not you who killed her."

"Well, I miss Sophea. We were separated for a long time. She wanted to pursue her career and went to India. The next time I knew about her. She was dead. I tried to contact her family but knew nothing. I got no clue that she had a sister or even a living mother."

"We never disclosed ourselves to anyone Arka. It was the condition of my mother. She has raised us and is very protective of us. Our father was killed by the Khmer Rouge in Cambodia. It was my mother who raised us in Tamil Nadu in Chennai. She had money to protect us from foxes hungry to feed upon us. Our uncle Sorya has stayed with us and shielded us for a long time. After he was gone, everyone claimed to be our living relation, initially, we were happy about having a family. But gradually we realized many of them learned of the wealth and lifestyle my mother had in Cambodia and are after the money. We had successfully lived away from those predators except for one, my uncle. Initially, he was good, he took care of us. Only later after Sorya's Uncle's death, we knew his real intention. He wanted to gain our wealth. At a point, my mother was okay to give him the needed wealth but when his married son wanted to marry my sister and tried to rape her when objected, my mother could not take it anymore. She made her boundaries to protect us. Our whereabouts were never disclosed. After the trauma, my mother sent my sister to Malaysia to study. I cannot blame you for what happened to her. But I wanted to find the truth and I found it. My uncle will be dealt with, we have men in India to settle that score but until then I need to ensure the safety of my Mom. In my family, we never lived happily till today from the day my father's death."

"I am sorry," Arka says.

"Can I ask you something ?"Tevy said.

"Yes"

"Do you still see my sister in me?"

"I do, which worries me, "I say.

"Get some rest Tevy" I hug Tevy awkwardly and go towards my car start it and drive along the Marina shore.

My phone flashes a message.

"Dinner at 8 PM? Orchard Street" Tevy's message

"I need a change of mood" I reply.

"So that is a no?"

"No, let us meet at the Clarke Quay bridge "I reply.

We meet on schedule and sit on the broad elevated area on the bridge. Strobe lights flash in every direction. Loud thumping music helped to break the coldness within us and lifted our spirits.

"Where is Priya?"I ask Tevy.

"She is at home."

"It would be boring for her to stay alone"

"I know, but she wanted us to have a date."

"Nice of her, I do not mind if she wanted to come here if you insist,"I say.

"I was looking forward to hearing that from you," She says.

"Let's grab a bottle of vodka, call her,"I say.

"Great," Tevy says as she dials in her phone.

After 30 minutes, Priya is with us. We had plain vodka with Tropicana Orange and Litchi. We hopped into all pubs and rummaged the dance floor. All of us are in a Tipsy mood.

"You should be careful Tevy," Priya says.

"Yes," I say.

"You should go to India as soon as possible,"Priya says.

I remain silent. Tevy looks at me. I jump over to the walking path and lit a cigarette.

"Priya," Tevy says trying to hush her.

Tevy walks toward me,

"I am sorry."

"No don't be sorry, it is for your own safety,"

"I cannot go without you."

"I love you," I say as I move back my head to say those words.

"I love you too," Tevy says as she kisses me softly on my lip.

We reported the incident to the Police in Singapore and Malaysia after she had left for India. A search was underway for Tevy's Uncle while his henchman is arrested in Singapore who did the attack on Priya's house.

I was in my flat in Malaysia, reading the newspaper and having coffee. The dark clouds were lurking to take over the purple ambient sky.

"You want a coffee?"A small whisper near my ear, the sound of Nila.

I startle and jump from my couch. After many months I hear her again, is it her?

"Yes, it is me."

"Nila, do not do this."

"You have taken good care of me. You loved me, I know you needed me, if not for my body, you have everything" Nila whispers.

I hear someone knocking on my door, softly but persistently.

"Do not open the door" Nila whispers.

I look through the peephole of five men dressed in suits like bouncers. Standing in the centre is a heavily built man with hair combed back and oversized rings on all his fingers.

As I wait the knocks get louder and harder.

I open the door.

"Hello Son," says the heavily built man

"Hi," I say with the door half open

"Can we come in ?"He says.

"I told you not to open the door" Nila whispers in my ear.

Hours later, I get a call on my mobile.

"I am leaving over the weekend for India," Tevy says.

"When will you be back? I ask.

"I want to meet you. I will take the flight to India from Malaysia," Tevy says.

"Today?"

"Yes"

"Alright, where?"

"I will come over to your place," Tevy says.

"Do not call her" whispers Tevy in my other ear as the phone line goes noisy in a moment.

"What? Are you there?"Tevy says as the line restores.

"There is a connection issue, I could not hear you."

"Okay, So?"

"So? What"

"Can I come over, my flight is tomorrow afternoon, I will meet you today before I leave?

"Okay,"I say hesitantly concerned about Nila's reactions.

"What time is your flight landing," I ask.

"Will message you the ticket details"

"Will pick you," I say.

Hot streaks of water jets hit the ground emanating an earthy smell. It was very rapid, short notice for people on the street to take shelter. The fruit vendors slide their sheets sheltering from the rain. A skinny lad with a watch bracelet like a Rolex on his wrist wearing a tee with a large font of Adidas walks like the rain has nothing to do with him. The boy with the balloon is walking past him. It was an unusually busy day only after the rain had started to pour restricting the mob to take shelter in patches as I see from the top.

Nila is roaming around in the house making it messy. I think she is angry about the arrival of Tevy. This is not expected, Nila is only coming back stronger every time. When I was small, I saw a woman who was killed by a ramming train while crossing a railway track. In a moment she is shattered all over. It pained me a lot to see. When I asked my uncle if they should retrieve her body from the track as rain is arriving. He said it didn't matter anymore. I asked why it didn't matter. He replied that she was dead, and the dead no longer feel anything. I thought he was right then. The dead do not feel anything. Maybe they do, they just do not have a body to express their feelings. Nila does not need a body.

I decided to check into a new hotel for the night. I pack my stuff and ignore Nila the best I can. I was able to evade her occasional throwing of things at me. I pick up a box of cigarettes and check for my ID, keys, glasses, and purse and I am out. Rest I can survive with and collect later.

I was early at the airport. I waited for thirty minutes for Tevy's flight to land. Even after landing an hour has passed and I am gazing at the passengers coming outside the airport like stars in the sky. There is no limit to the stars. I could think of the north star as Tevy, however, the north is easily noticeable but not Tevy. I could see the silhouette of Tevy walking towards me only to be lit by the lights of the luggage belt. She is smiling at me. It has been a few weeks only but seems like years since I have seen her. She lost a lot of weight. Every passing minute is an hour. I think this is the common feeling when someone waits for their loved ones. Tevy walks out and I forget whatever has happened and we both embrace with stretched arms, and I hug her. We walk towards the taxi stand, but I do not feel like going home nor does Tevy. She is carrying just a bag. We walk over to the open-roof pub.

"Two Ale," I order.

"Was I late?" Tevy asks.

"Not really"

Due to the heat water sprinkles are used to splash bursts cooling down the air around us. The plants beside us moved to the wind from the fans. The mood was immediately improved after a sip of ale.

"I wanted to come to Singapore actually."

"Why?"

"Clarke Quay"

"Ya it was a wonderful day" Tevy smiles at me.

We order french fries and steak.

"What next," I ask.

"I want to get drunk today," says Tevy.

"Are you sure?"

"At least, I want to try all the flavours of beer here."

"Lager to Strong," I ask.

"We started with an ale, so we are mid way" Tevy smiles.

"Tevy there is something I have to tell you"

"If it will upset me, don't say it," Tevy says.

I was going to reveal about Nila but hesitantly remained silent. For that matter even I wanted to drink a lot.

After a few drinks, we played darts. Tevy hit the bull's eye and won. Everyone around is so high that they started to celebrate laughing incessantly like mad.

Tevy played with other women, while I was drinking with their partners. He is less spoken than I am. We said Hi and resorted to our drinks once in a while cheering our ladies.

We hopped places and went to Chinatown. Went through malls swaying around holding each other. I brought a printed tee and a gold Tissot prx to go with it, I wanted to buy the automatic but the dial of the quartz was loved by Tevy. I purchased perfumes and souvenirs for Tevy along with a Longines watch which I discreetly purchased. We walked out of the store and came to a garden top in Chinatown. I asked for her hand and knelt on my knee put forth the watch on her hand and asked her if she would marry me. I had combined that with a ceramic ring, which I managed to steal while walking to the top I-do not think it would cost more than a fifty but I had no time to find a good one.

"I hereby take you as my wife, excuse the ring it will be replaced,"I say as I band the watch to her wrist and place the ring.

"I love the ring," She says and kisses me.

I have never been anything close to this romantic in my life.

The people around us are equally crazy today. They started to clap at us. We hold each other tight and walk around. We reached home around 2 AM in the night.

At 4 PM the following day, I hear a knock on my hotel door. I walk towards the door and open it.

"Place your hands up,"Four policemen on duty with batons at their waists and revolver pointed at me, walk inside, they handcuff me.

"You are arrested for choking your friend Tevy and causing death, if you wish to say anything you can later in an hour, can you confirm if you are Arka and ID please."

"I am," I say.

CHAPTER ELEVEN

2016 Singapore

Narrator: Arka

We reached home late in the night. Lights are off in the apartment, which could be due to a power outage.

"Why the generator is not on?" I ask the security.

He does not reply and walks away murmuring something to himself.

"What's wrong with you?"

No reply.

Tevy is drunk and walking semi-consciously as I hold her hand.

"Did we reach?"

"Yes we did," I say.

I light my zippo and walk the stairs towards my floor and the room. As I enter the room, the crocket is moving gently while the glasses in it are vibrating heavily.

On the cupboard, there is a text written with a marker "I hate you,"

I think Nila is mad at me. I put Tevy in the bed and go to the kitchen to fetch a bottle of water.

The kitchen door gets locked from the outside.

"Nila stop it, do not be stupid,"I say.

I could hear the screams of Tevy.

I bang on the door and after the third try it opens. Tevy is sleeping on the bed. I walk towards her.

"Are you alright?"I ask.

"Why? What happened?"She says.

I do not say anything.

"Make yourself comfortable," I say.

The wind started to churn outside the window and spiralled inside like a mini tornado.

"Nila! Stop this can you come over to the balcony," I say.

I pick a scramble board and move there.

"What is it you want?"I say.

The plastic letter blocks started to move on the floor.

"You" Nila arranges the words in reply.

"Okay, how to want me, I am alive?"

"You are not" She arranges the scramble.

"Please be practical, I am not buried, I have a body," I say.

"Did you love me?"Nila asks.

"Of course I did Nila"

For the next few hours, things in the house began to levitate and fall. With Nila this is usual, luckily Tevy is quite unconscious that she cannot fear Nila as she cannot see or feel anything.

I drink bourbon straight for a few minutes, sip water and go to bed.

I could hear a few pieces of glassware dismissed to the ground by Nila and a fan on the ceiling moving at a speed unusually rapid even without power.

In the middle of the night, I hear a whisper.

"Please Arka, why are you fooling yourself?"

"What is it?" I say.

"Whatever you see is not real just like your dream now. You

may have strong emotions now but trust me. You will wake up from your dreams. One day when you wake up, you will find you have nobody. On that day you will realize you do not need a nose to smell, a tongue to taste or fulfil your desires with your body. Did it occur to you without a body to please me how is that I am still bonded to you? The word "Love" used and abused in your world is not the same word I do. You must be blessed to have me. Trust me once, and I will tell you the secrets which sages have given all their years and did not find it. Scientists have tried and failed but never could find the exact reason for the aftermath of life and energy after death. I know many things Arka much beyond your imagination. I am faster than the speed of light or the power of thought. I always gave you the freedom Arka to let you think. It takes a minute to take you in my control. Your mind is like a spoon to me. I can handle it yet I am not always. What you are seeking cannot last Arka it is superficial."

"What is that you want now?" I ask,

"Come to me, endure the suffering for a few minutes, I will show you the path to absolute love,"Nila whispers.

"I cannot trust you,"I say.

"Forget the past Arka. I had a superficial mind and body. I wanted you for a lot of reasons which are not significant to me now. What matters are that I can communicate with only you. Do you not see how miraculous is this? This is something even I cannot ignore if I want to. Maybe there is something more to the foolishness in my love for you."Nila whispers

"You want me to die."

"Practically yes, but in truth, you live by dying," Nila says as she moves nearer to me holding the pillow positioned across my face a few inches away.

"Stop it, Nila, stop it" My voice goes muffled as I try to resist her choking me with a pillow.

My voice goes muffled as she puts supernatural pressure. This is not something a woman in human form can do. I try hard and push back onto her.

"Stop it" Nila screams.

I push back Nila with the same pillow onto her beside my bed, my hands stuffed with the pillow onto her face as hard as I can. After a few struggling moments, she stops to resist, she freed me for now.

After a few hours, I wake up and walk over to drink some water. I was sweating profusely. This was an intense moment of relief after what I had gone through. The dream was so real, I could feel Nila as she was when alive. The lights are out with one of the bulbs breaking to the floor. She tried to kill me but how can I die in a dream? I fetch Tropicana tracing to the fridge in the dark and walk towards my bed. Sleep is far away at least for a while now. I place a pillow underneath my thighs for comfort and sleep on my dorsal side and close my eyes taking a deep breath. Tevy rests beside me, comfortably asleep. I need to talk to her tomorrow about Nila.

"I will die but will not give up Tevy" I whisper to Nila as I fall asleep gradually.

www.ingramcontent.com/pod-product-compliance
Lightning Source LLC
LaVergne TN
LVHW091303150826
845673LV00006B/1519

* 9 7 9 8 8 9 0 6 6 4 7 2 3 *